Full Figured 4:
Carl Weber Presents

Full Figured 4:
Carl Weber Presents

Anna J. and Natalie Weber

www.urbanbooks.net

Urban Books, LLC
78 East Industry Court
Deer Park, NY 11729

ISBN 13: 978-1-60162-377-5
ISBN 10: 1-60162-377-1

First Mass Market Printing May 2013
First Trade Paperback Printing December 2011
Printed in the United States of America

10 9 8 7 6 5 4 3 2 1

This is a work of fiction. Any references or similarities to actual events, real people, living or dead, or to real locales are intended to give the novel a sense of reality. Any similarity in other names, characters, places, and incidents is entirely coincidental.

Distributed by Kensington Publishing Corp.
Submit Wholesale Orders to:
Kensington Publishing Corp.
C/O Penguin Group (USA) Inc.
Attention: Order Processing
405 Murray Hill Parkway
East Rutherford, NJ 07073-2316
Phone: 1-800-526-0275
Fax: 1-800-227-9604

Full Figured 4:
Carl Weber Presents

by

Anna J. and Natalie Weber

Someone Else's Guy

by

Anna J.

I can't get off my high horse and I can't let go
You are the one who makes me feel so real
What am I supposed to do when I'm hooked on you
Then I realize that you're somebody else's guy . . .

~ "Somebody Else's Guy": Jocelyn Brown
(1984)

10 Seconds

*You did me wrong for the last time. And I
took so much from you baby, but you really
crossed the line. . . .*

~Jazmine Sullivan

It felt like I was moving in slow motion as I
parked my car down the block and tiptoed carefully up to our gravel driveway. Something just
didn't sit right in my spirit when I drove past our
house and saw my husband's Mercedes parked
in the driveway. He'd said he would be away on
business when I left this morning, and normally
when he was away, he would park his car inside
of the garage space he'd rented near the airport.
I'd had to double back to get a case of hair color
that had come in over the weekend, and I knew I
would need one of the colors for my three o'clock
appointment. That was the only reason I'd left
the shop.

In my heart I was hoping he had only left some papers and had doubled back, just as I had, to get them. Still, something didn't sit right. Wishing I had parked a little closer, I struggled as I hefted my pear-shaped frame up the steep hill and through the grass so that he wouldn't hear the rocks crunching under my feet. Sweat began to pour down the sides of my chubby face, and my heart began to beat faster the closer I got to the back door.

Leaning against the door to catch my breath, I peered through the sheer curtain covering the window, hoping I wouldn't see anything I would regret. Nothing looked out of the norm, so I proceeded with caution as I quietly opened the door and crept into my home. A Victorian-style Tudor that sat way back off the street, with a horseshoe driveway and fourteen-carat-gold door handles attached to French doors. My dream home, which Sean hadn't hesitated having built for me from the ground up. Out of the corner of my eye I saw Sean's keys resting on the countertop, and I figured that he had indeed left something. He was so anal about everything being in its proper place, so he would have never just left his keys there unless he was in a rush.

Something told me to just grab my case of hair color and go, but I didn't want him to catch me going back out, and have to face being questioned about why I'd parked down the block. I already had an excuse; I'd just tell him I was exercising. He had been in my face about my weight for a while now, and I knew if I didn't get it together in a hurry, I would eventually lose him. Still, it was hard to stick to a meal plan when I was standing behind the chair all day. Some days I barely got to eat, and when I finally did sit down to a meal, it was on. Who wanted a salad when they hadn't eaten all day? Damn that! Give me a rack of ribs and a chocolate shake to wash it down with.

As I sidestepped into the living room, my feet sank into the plush carpeting, which we'd paid way too much for, but which matched perfectly the Egyptian tile that lay in the foyer. Sean wanted me to have the best of everything, and no expense had been spared—I put quite a dent in his checkbook—to furnish our place. As I rounded the winding staircase and came face-to-face with my wedding gown, encased in a glass frame that had been built into the wall, I remembered that day so vividly and wished, for a second, that I could get back down to that size eleven.

Everything was in fast-forward when Sean and I first hooked up. I had just opened my little salon near the King of Prussia Mall, closer to where the movie theater was located, and I was hoping that the few black folks that lived around there would patronize me. It had seemed like a great location at the time, and I had had high hopes about stepping out on my own and doing what I wanted to do. Business was slow at first, and I thought about closing up shop for good. When the one and only Patti LaBelle walked into my shop because her stylist was battling the flu, I felt like I was given a second chance to start fresh. She needed to get touched up for a television appearance, and I knew my thoughts about closing the shop were out the door. After getting over being starstruck, I did the damn thing to Patti's hair, and had been on the rise ever since.

I was called to do, in a crunch, the hair of some of the brightest stars on the scene, such as Nia Long and Chrisette Michele, and pretty soon I built a name for myself. I was ready for the big leagues and was introduced to Sean while out at a mixer. He was a stockbroker and came highly recommended by everyone. I thought he would be a stiff shirt, wanting to talk to me only about investing my money, but I came to find out, he was really down to earth. After months of dating and jet setting, he popped the question. No, I didn't have as much cash as he did, but I wasn't broke, so why not? I made it clear that I wasn't signing a prenuptial under any circumstances, and he was cool with it, so we moved forward. That seemed like so long ago, and I don't know what had happened over the years, but I missed the Sean I used to know.

Sniffing back tears, I rounded the stairs and took the back steps leading to his office. Sliding along the wall, I moved like a cheetah stalking its prey as I crept up on the door, an overweight cheetah, but a cheetah nonetheless. I didn't hear anything as I pressed my ear against the door and turned the knob slowly. Opening the door to a dark office, I breathed a temporary sigh of relief when I found it vacant. That relief was short lived because I had yet to get to the upstairs. Since I was downstairs, I checked the game room and the exercise room, finding them both empty.

Light on my feet, I took the stairs two at a time, being sure to skip the third step, which creaked when you stepped on it. Back at ground level, I took a second to get my breathing in order, vowing to hit up the treadmill in the morning. As I made my way slowly up the staircase, I noticed that my bedroom door was cracked open. Sean hated open doors, and I wondered if I had left it open or if he had. Or maybe there was a robber on the other side? Who was I kidding? Something just didn't seem right, and a woman's intuition never failed.

Looking around for a weapon, all I saw was my crystal Tiffany lotus lamp, which cost way too much to break over someone's head, but I grabbed it, anyway. Sean would just have to buy me another one. It seemed like my entire life flashed through my mind as I made my way down the hallway. That was when I heard it, another woman's voice, more like a moan, escaping from the crack in my bedroom door. Maybe I was tripping. . . . There was no way. I stopped for a minute and shook my head back and forth. I knew I didn't just hear what I thought I heard.

Inching closer, I heard it again. Okay, so maybe Sean had come home, and he was in the bedroom, watching a porno. It had been a few months since our bedroom walls had had something to talk about, and maybe he needed a release. The extra weight I had put on turned him off, and it had got to the point where he didn't want to sleep in the same bed with me, one more reason to tackle that treadmill in the morning. Still inching closer, I heard it again, but this time the voice sounded familiar.

"You want Daddy to go deeper?" I heard my husband ask in a husky voice that he used only when we were making love.

"Yes, Daddy, go deeper," the voice responded, halting my steps immediately. Was I dreaming? There was no way. . . .

"Hold it open for me. Damn, you feel good."

It was like the earth had stopped rotating and all the sound in the universe had been sucked out. I could not believe what I just heard. There was no way my husband and his assistant were in my bed! He'd said he hated a skinny woman, but he definitely didn't want me at the size I was. He'd said a skinny chick could only take notes for him, because she damn sure wouldn't eat anything. Would he really do this to me?

I couldn't take it anymore, and as I eased my bedroom door open, I couldn't believe my eyes. Stretched out on my cream linen spread with her chicken legs pointed to the ceiling was Sean's assistant, Carla, with my husband balls deep inside of her. He looked like he was trying to climb inside of her as he used his well-manicured toes to get a good grip on the edge of the bed so that he could, indeed, push deeper. I was instantly sick to my stomach.

The happy couple didn't even notice me standing in the doorway. My husband's head was thrown back in ecstasy, and his eyes were squeezed so tight, his expression looked more like a grimace from the side. Carla's mouth formed a wide O as her small breasts bounced up and down to the motion of my husband's ocean. They sounded like two savage beasts as I watched her claw at his back.

He used one hand to balance himself as the other firmly gripped her side. This shit was crazy. It felt like I was standing there forever as the scent of her vagina blanketed the air around me. The sounds in the room seemed to intensify by a million, and I could've sworn I heard her juices slurping as my husband pushed in and pulled out.

The lamp seemed to weigh a ton as I raised it over my head and aimed it at the headboard, throwing it full force across the room. The loud crash startled even me as the lamp made contact with the wall, and crystal shards covered both of their naked bodies. Sean jumped up from the bed with a rock-hard dick swinging in the air. Carla scrambled to cover her naked body with my new linen spread as I snapped and began tossing expensive bottles of cologne and perfume from the dresser, the bottles breaking as they hit the wall. The different fragrances mixing with the aroma of sex in the room made me feel nauseous, and through my blurred vision I tried to aim at both of their heads, hoping to knock the hell out of at least one of them.

This was not happening to me again! We took vows for better or for worse, in sickness and in health, 'til death. It was too bad one of us would have to die today, and it wasn't going to be me. I rummaged through the middle drawer of my princess wicker dresser for the pistol I kept there, not thinking anything about the years I would spend in jail if I actually pulled the trigger. I didn't deserve this. I was a good wife to him.

"Valencia, you don't want to do this. I can explain," Sean began as he inched his way toward me, dick still hard and smeared with her juices. This trifling-ass man didn't even have the decency to use a condom.

"Take one more step and your left ball sack is history," I said with venom in my voice as I wiped tears and snot away from my face. I loved this man's dirty drawers, flaws and all, and this was how it ended up for me?

"Valencia, please put the—" Shots rang out, landing just above Carla's head, putting two holes in the wall, halting her speech immediately.

"I missed on purpose," I said in her direction, never taking my eyes off of my husband.

"Valencia, let me explain. It's not what you think. I was just—"

"Your dick is still hard. That's amazing all in itself, since you could never stay up for more than three minutes with me," I spat, cutting him off. I couldn't believe he had the audacity to try and explain this shit.

"Honey, I just want to—"

"You both have ten seconds to get the fuck out of my house, or the shots start again. One . . ."

"Valencia, you're being irrational. If you hadn't gained all of that weight . . . ," my husband pleaded with me as he searched the room for his pants.

"Two . . ."

"Baby, just hear me out. I don't care anything about her."

"Three . . ." I spoke in a cool tone, sending a shot to the ceiling to let these fools know I wasn't playing. It was about to go down up in this piece if they didn't move faster.

"Four . . ."

Carla leaped from the bed and haphazardly threw her sundress over her head, leaving her bra and panties in a crumpled heap on the floor. She made a mad dash for her purse just as Sean was stepping, his bottom bare, into his silk slacks. Aiming the gun toward them both, I got a shot off that whizzed between them and landed in the center of our wedding picture, the one that we'd had hand drawn by a prominent artist out of Newark. It was such a memorable night.

"Six . . . ," I barked, purposely skipping five to speed their asses up. I couldn't stand the sight of either one of them.

Both Sean and Carla inched past me and ran for their lives out the back of the house. I heard

Sean's car start, then shriek out of the driveway, kicking up gravel in its haste. I was like a mannequin as I stood in silence, taking in the scene of the crime. Every man that I'd ever loved had done the same damn thing. Either they cheated on me or I came to find out I was the jump-off from the door. Why did this always have to happen to me?

I took a seat at the overpriced vanity table that Sean got me for my birthday last year; it wasn't until then that I fully allowed my tears to flow. What a mess my life had become in a matter of minutes. Now I had to find a way to put the pieces back together. I just wasn't sure if there was a way to do it, or if I wanted to, for that matter.

Fairy Tales

*She spoke about happy endings, of stories
not like this. She said he'd slay all dragons,
defeat the evil prince. . . .*

~Anita Baker

I sat in a daze for what felt like forever, until
the shrill ringing of my house phone brought me
out of my astonished state. Looking toward the
nightstand, I hated the thought of even going
near the bed I used to share with my husband.
After all, there was no way I could occupy that
space after what I saw today. I could still see
them disrespecting our vows right before my
eyes, and I could feel my anger rising again. My
first instinct was to finish tearing the room up,
but what good would that do?

Taking another route, I dragged my exhausted
body to the back room where my office was, and
answered the phone there. Plopping down in the
chair, I used what little energy I had left to pick

up the receiver, peeping the caller ID before doing so. There was no way I would talk to Sean right now. I just hoped I wouldn't kill his trifling ass the next time I saw him.

Satisfied that it wasn't Sean, I picked the phone up, only to hear Terrell, my close friend and the top stylist at my shop, asking where I was. He had been calling my cell phone for the last hour, and it wasn't until I heard his voice that I realized how much time had gone by. It was already two thirty, and my three o'clock had arrived early. My cell phone was on the passenger seat of my car. I didn't think about bringing it in at the time, because I was supposed to be just running in to get my box and jetting back out. Boy, was I wrong.

"T, I need you to take care of my clients for the rest of the day. You are not going to believe what just happened."

After I ran down the entire scenario and answered the questions that he had, I was finally off the phone a half hour later and back at square one. What was my next step? Sean and I were seven years into our marriage. How did you start over after that? I knew back then that I needed a plan B, or even another plan A, but I didn't think I would need it this soon. My head was spinning. I mean, I had my own thing going on with running my shop, but I was married. 'Til death did us part.

Before Sean, I was simply Valencia McCoy, owner of the Real McCoy Salon Experience. I never thought about getting married. I was just trying to maintain after walking away from years in corporate America to be an entrepreneur. It took me only two years to clear up my credit and stack my chips, and then I was able to land a space for my shop without having to take out a loan. I had the first year's rent in the bank, plus extra, and I was ready to make it work.

I started thinking again about how a year and a half after opening the shop and getting things going, things started to get a little crazy, and I wasn't building my client base up like I needed to. I was making okay money, but my stash was getting low, and I was just making enough to pay the rent and bills. To be honest, I was dreading having to get back behind a desk, but I had a mortgage to maintain, and I refused to go back to my momma's house.

On the very day that I decided it was time to close the doors, the limousine with Patti LaBelle pulled up in front of my shop. I was thinking to myself that maybe I had finally won the Publishers Clearing House Sweepstakes, and Ed McMahon had come to run my money. I had already packed up most of the shop at that point, and one couldn't tell whether I was moving in or out, because there were boxes everywhere. Part of the problem was I couldn't find reliable stylists to fill the other chairs. I took a glance in the mirror. I had to make sure my hair was straight and my lip gloss was popping for my big TV debut.

I noticed two big and burly men get out of the limo and wondered when Ed had started running with security. Or, maybe this was the part they didn't show on TV. Watching intently, and practicing my surprised reaction in my head, I noticed a woman exit the vehicle with bug-eyed glasses and a huge hat covering her head. Okay, this was some new shit, but I was ready to roll with it.

One of the guards walked in the front, and one in the back, and that was when it dawned on me that this wasn't Ed McMahon, and I wasn't about to make a major come up. Resting my body back in my chair, I prepared myself to tell this person that my shop was closed for business. I had packed everything away, and I really didn't know where anything was, so even if I wanted to make that last couple of bucks before I shut the doors forever, I couldn't.

"I'm sorry. I'm closed for business," I said to the trio as they entered the salon. The guy in the front acted like he didn't hear a word I said, and my face was on a fast track to a frown until the woman walked in. She gracefully removed her glasses, and I almost hit the floor when I realized it was none other than Patti LaBelle standing in my doorway.

"Honey, you might want to open back up. I have an emergency, and you are the only shop open right now that can fix it. I have to be in front of the camera in three hours."

I was stuck on stupid, to say the least. Here I was, praying for a come up, and I had just come up in a major way. Patti LaBelle was standing in my shop, and I was stuck with my mouth open.

"Okay, let's get started. What do you want done?" I responded, coming to my senses quickly and ungluing my feet from the floor.

I jumped up and began searching through the million or so boxes so that I could at least get started. I had an entire case of Indian Remy hair that I knew she would love, and so many styles flowed through my head as I searched around. Would she want something slick and chic, or would she want something wild and crazy? Patti was so versatile, you just never knew what to expect from her. I couldn't believe I had got an opportunity like this, and I knew that after today I would be unpacking my boxes for good. I had to give it another shot.

We chatted like old friends as we searched through hair magazines and came up with a style that she loved. I even used some of my specially made hair products, and everything flowed naturally. Patti was so warm and inviting, and by the time I turned her chair toward the mirror and added my finishing touches, we had exchanged numbers, and she'd promised to send me some business. On top of all that, she paid me three times the amount I was charging her, and shouted out my salon information during her interview.

My shop door was in full swing after that, and pretty soon I had way more clients than I could handle. See how God works? I had to call in some reinforcements, and it didn't take a lot to convince my bestest buddy since forever to take a chair. After the grueling task of finding another stylist with a license, we finally added Shay to the team, and it was straight to the top from there. Within that year I hired a masseuse and a manicurist, and it was a full spa experience behind those doors. Not only could you get fried, dyed, and laid to the side, you could also get pampered with a relaxing massage, among other things. We were waxing and plucking and all that jazz.

I was enjoying the boost my shop got, and I was able to stack up some major cash in the process. Life was good, finally, and it got even better when I was invited by Jill Scott to an invite-only mixer that was being held in Olde City. I met her at a hair show I was attending where she was the opening act, and I was able to slip her my card on the low. She came to my shop a few times when she was home in Philly, and we got to be real cool. When she invited me out to the mixer, there was no way I could say no. I took an entire day and cleared my book so that I could be ready. Terrell made sure my hair was fabulous after I had a relaxing massage and a brown sugar facial. Tisha, my manicurist, got my feet and hands together, and I got dressed at the shop to make sure my outfit was on point. At that time I was a tight size eleven, with an ample ass and perfect breasts. Those were the days.

I was killing them softly when I stepped into the party. I rushed over to Jill when I saw her. I had done her hair the day before, and she told me to have plenty of business cards with me at the party. It was a nice crowd of celebrities and others who were powerful on the back end of the business. John Legend, Musiq Soulchild, and a few others were in the building, doing their thing. I had to take a chill pill for a second after doing the Dougie with Alicia Keys on the dance floor. Still smiling, I walked up to the bar to order a Coke; I'd had one drink already, and that was my limit. Drunk driving was not my thing. Besides, the Aston Martin I had rented needed to be back to the dealer in one piece, so I wasn't taking any chances.

"Can I have a Coke please?" I leaned over and asked the bartender over the loud music. On the lean back a fine-ass man caught my attention, and I had to keep myself from staring. I had obviously caught his, too, because he smiled at me. When the bartender brought my drink over, he said it had been paid for by my admirer. I mouthed a thank-you his way, turning my back to the bar. As I sipped, I looked out on the crowd, feeling great. I could definitely get used to this! I had passed out a lot of business cards to celebrities and models as well, hoping it would drum up more business. My salon was doing great, but new business was always good.

"So, how are you enjoying the festivities?" said a smooth, deep voice from the side. I turned to see the guy from the end of the bar standing at my side, and he was even more gorgeous up close. *Damn.*

"I'm having a great time so far. You?" I flirted a little, still people watching, scouting potential new clients.

"It seems like my night might have just gotten a little better. Care to dance?" he asked as the beginnings of "Cupid Shuffle" began to flow through the speakers and a crowd started to form on the dance floor. I gulped down the rest of my Coke and joined everyone on the floor. We two-stepped and dropped it low for hours. I hadn't had that much fun in a good long time.

As the night came to an end, I passed out the last of my business cards. After saying my good-byes and snapping a few pictures of my favorite celebs, I gathered myself to make my way to my car. On the way out I rode the elevator down with Jill and Alicia. We chatted about the night we'd just had. Alicia Keys gave me a warm hug, and I stood out front chatting with Jill as we waited for the valet to bring our cars around.

"I saw you kicking it with Sean. That's a good catch, girl," Jill joked with me.

"Is he? Who is he, exactly?" I questioned seriously. He was kinda fly and had seemed interested.

"He's a stockbroker and handles finances for a ton of celebs. He's been single for a while, too, and can be kind of shy. Don't sleep on that number, girl," she replied just as her car was pulling up. We embraced once more before she got in her car and left.

I was still waiting for my car to come around. Just as I was starting to get impatient, I heard that smooth voice again, causing a smile to involuntarily spread across my face.

"You didn't leave a glass slipper behind, so I didn't know how I would find you. I was so sad," Sean joked as he stood next to me.

"I see you were able to catch up."

"Yeah, I was hoping we could find a late-night breakfast spot where we can actually talk and not have to holler over the music."

"I don't go out with strangers," I joked with him as I prepared to get in my ride. It was the next car in line to be pulled to the door.

"I'm not a stranger. You taught me how to Dougie. That makes us friends now." He smiled as I walked around to the other side. "That's my car behind yours. Are you hungry?"

"Sure. Follow me," I responded, giving in a little too easily. I mean, it was just breakfast. What harm could be done from sharing the most important meal of the day with a handsome new friend? Sean didn't even wait for the valet to drive all the way up to the door. He ran and hopped in his car and followed me down to a greasy spoon not too far up the road. Things had been going great in my life this year, and I was hoping Sean might be the icing on the cake.

Rocket Love

*You took me riding in your rocket, gave me
a star, but at a half a mile from heaven you
dropped me back down to this cold, cold
world. . . .*

~Stevie Wonder

"Valencia, are you going to let me explain?"
Sean asked and had the nerve to have an attitude.

*Men. I swear they don't have the sense that
God gave them.*

"There's nothing to explain, Sean. I know
what I saw, and it's a done deal. You wanted
skinny, you got it. Do you."

"I really wish you would let me get a word in
edgewise," he said, more frustrated than he'd
been in the beginning.

Like I give a flying rat's ass.

"And I really wish something had happened to
me that caused me to have short-term memory
loss. That way it would be like I never met you."

The phone line went quiet for a minute, and I allowed him the time to let my last statement sink in. Okay, so I'd gained weight. In a marriage you worked through the problems. You didn't bring in more issues. Not that I would have felt any differently had he been cheating with another fat chick, but to have someone I knew in my damn bed was unacceptable. She'd broken bread in my house and everything. I knew there was something about her that had never really set well with me, and I came to find out it was because she had a thing for my husband. Well, my possible ex-husband. I didn't know how we were going to get through this one.

"Was that necessary?"

"Was you sleeping with your assistant in our bed necessary? Wait. There wasn't any sleeping going on, so I guess that doesn't constitute y'all actually sleeping together."

"Valencia, seriously. I can't deal with this today. When I get back from handling business, we'll talk about this. You act like you didn't push me out the door."

Now it was my turn to be stunned into silence. Did this man just blame me for his infidelity? What was the world coming to? True, he had been on my ass for a good minute about my weight steadily going up. The crazy shit was, I didn't really pay it that much attention. I wore sweats most of the time, so when they got a little too tight, I just went out and got a bigger size, blaming the tight fit on dryer shrinkage. It was not like I was depressed or harboring some deep, dark childhood secret that had me ballooning out of control, like most folks that attached that stigma to their weight problems. I was on the go and didn't always make the best food choices— simple as that.

Okay, so who knew that three too many half gallons of Turkey Hill butter pecan and daily trips to Cold Stone Creamery during the summer would have me tipping the scale? Those mix-ins had me hooked! The life of a hairstylist was brutal, with long hours and trying to please the public. I'd admit I let myself go a little bit, but was it that serious? My life was on fast-forward, and we all ate on the go. Clients could get a little testy when they felt like you were taking a break and they had been sitting for a while.

No one could have ever told me that Sean and I would be at this point. Ours had been like a whirlwind romance right off the pages of Harlequin. We sat in the diner for hours, and I felt like I was catching up with an old friend. We had so much in common, and he made me laugh. I hadn't laughed in a long time, after swearing off men to start my path to independence. My ex-boyfriend was a dumb ass, and I wasn't in a rush to relive that kind of life with anyone else.

"So, how did you learn how to Dougie?" he asked me as we shared an ice cream sundae covered in hot fudge. We both had an undeniable sweet tooth and found that fact to be a plus.

"I don't know." I blushed a little as I continued to eat. "Watching videos at the shop, I guess. I've always had a nice rhythm, though."

"Oh yeah, I can see that," he responded, looking me up and down.

This man was looking good and smelling even better. I had to pep talk myself into keeping my panties on and going straight home afterward.

"So you saying you really know how to move?" he asked.

"I'm saying I can hold my own," I replied, flirting back.

"Well, listen," he began after checking the time on a nice Franck Muller wrist piece. This man had money and good taste. "It's seven in the morning, and I'm already running behind the times. There's a sexy little salsa spot in Jersey that is always jumping on Saturday nights. Can I get some of your time next weekend?"

He was right about having to get a move on. I had a standing eight o'clock appointment that always showed up a half hour early, so I needed to be there on time. I had just enough time to jet home, shower and change, and make it the shop to get Ms. Jackson curled and back out the door. His offer sounded tempting, but of course, it would only be fitting to play a little hard to get since I gave in to breakfast so easily.

"I'll contact you this week, once I see what my schedule looks like. Is that cool?"

"That's wonderful."

Both of us gathered our stuff up, and I discreetly slipped my shoes back on, as I had come out of them during our meal. I sashayed in front of him, working the hell out of the silk wrap dress I was wearing. He was such the gentleman as he rushed to open the door for me. We slowly walked to my car, and I really didn't want our time to end.

"Okay, princess, get home safe and enjoy your Saturday. Don't work too hard," he said into my ear as we embraced tightly. Damn, it felt good being in his arms. It had been a minute since I'd been held like that, and I was a little reluctant to let go. As we stepped back, he planted the softest kiss in the world on my forehead, which almost had me laid out, but your girl held it together. I had to represent.

We said our good-byes, and once I was securely in my car, he turned and got inside of his, and we were off. It was already quarter after seven by then, so I had to settle for just removing my makeup and throwing on some sweats so that I could hurry to the shop. I'd have my assistant take the rental car back later. I was smiling all the way to the shop, and no matter how hard I tried, I couldn't wipe the smile from my face. As I glanced at his business card on the dash, I reminded my- self to stick it in my pocketbook before I forgot. I wanted to get to know Sean . . . definitely.

"Diva!" Terrell shouted out to me as I walked into the shop. I was still smiling and couldn't wait to update them on my night. "Diva, do spill all the juicy details!"

"Let me take care of Ms. Jackson, and I'll tell you everything. Let her know that I'm ready."

I had gotten to the shop five minutes late, and Ms. Jackson, although a faithful client, was extra impatient and I needed to get her out the door. I didn't know what caused her to be so ornery, and she wasn't an old woman, by any means. I whipped her up in record time, and after enter- ing her appointment for next Saturday morning in my book, I had time to sit and dish the dirt.

Over breakfast I ran down the entire night to the crew, making sure to leave nothing out. Sean had me wondering, and I was hoping next Saturday would get here soon. I hadn't really been out to enjoy myself in a minute with the shop picking up business the way it had, and my book almost doubling in a matter of months. I was thinking about adding a barber to the mix, and I wanted to redecorate, so every free moment I had was spent getting my shop where I needed it to be. A little "man-tainment" was well overdue!

"He called you princess?" Terrell blushed as he sat, wide-eyed, listening to my story. "Girl, I'm in love for you! What does he do for a living?"

"Apparently, he's someone to reckon with. All the people at the party said he was a good catch," I replied as I pulled his card out to show them. It was like winning the golden ticket to get into the chocolate factory. Everyone was in awe.

"Wait." Terrell got up and took the card from my hand. "Are you telling me that you just had breakfast with Sean King, stockbroker to the stars?"

"I guess so. At least, that was the word at the party. Why?"

"Girl, do you know who he is?" Terrell asked, looking like I had just hit Powerball.

"Well, the card says he's a stockbroker, and everyone has confirmed it. Why are you so amped up about it?"

Instead of responding, he went to the computer and quickly began to type something in Google. We all gathered around like it was story time, waiting for the screen to display the answers. I came to find out, Sean was a heavy hitter and was known all over the globe for helping people stay millionaires. He worked only with A-list celebs, and apparently even Oprah trusted him with her money. There was a little mess with a bad breakup he endured a few years back, but other than that, he seemed like a pretty clean-cut dude. I was very, very impressed.

"Girl, seems like you might have hit the jackpot," Terrell finally said as we backed away from the computer to tend to our clients.

"Maybe, maybe not. We're supposed to be hooking up on Saturday to go salsa dancing, so I guess we'll see where it goes from there, if it goes anywhere at all. Hell, we just met last night," I responded, more to bring myself down than to appease the crowd. Sean was nice, but he was on the go. I was more of a stationary kind of person, so I didn't know how that would work out. It was nice that he was paid, but I had my own money, so his was a non-issue. I wasn't putting all my eggs in one basket, and I really wasn't even sure I was ready to start dating yet, so we would see.

I busied myself at my station, and it felt like the day zoomed by. I was glad that the Aston

Martin dealer had a service that would come and get the car, so I didn't have to have my assistant return it. The shop was rocking today, and I honestly didn't think that anyone would have time to leave. We hardly had a chance to eat but managed to share a pepperoni pizza in between frying and dying. I'd prayed for the day that my shop would be bumping like this, so I had no complaints.

A deliveryman appeared in our doorway with a huge bouquet of tiger lilies in his hands. "I have a delivery for Ms. McCoy," he announced.

I couldn't believe it, and it was like the entire shop came to a screeching halt. Walking to the front, I signed for the delivery and sat the vase down on the receptionist's desk. Searching for the card, I finally found it, wrapped in a burnt orange ribbon on the other side.

"Who is it from?" Terrell asked the question that everyone wanted answered.

"It's from Sean." I blushed as I read the card out loud. "Princess, make sure you're ready to dance on Saturday. Missing you already. Sean."

"Awwww . . . ," came a collective sigh from the shop.

I was smiling from ear to ear and could hardly concentrate for the rest of the day. I wanted to call him right then, but I figured I'd give him a buzz once I got home and settled. I didn't want him to think I was sweating him or anything like that. He did get cool points for remembering that I told him tiger lilies were my favorite. Sean had me riding on a rocket, and I hoped my feet wouldn't hit the ground anytime soon.

It was definitely a productive day at the Real McCoy Salon Experience. So much so, we decided to go and get some drinks before calling it a night. After cleaning up my station, I dashed home to shower and change, while Terrell and Shay finished up their last clients. I wanted to call Sean, but he was probably out wheeling and dealing, and he had mentioned having to fly out to Cali, and they were a few hours behind us.

He definitely put a smile on my face, and I couldn't wait to find out more about this mystery man. After shutting down the Internet and checking my appearance once more in the mirror, I decided I was happy with my outfit and it was time to hit the dance floor. You got to live only once, and from here on out I was living my life like it was golden!

Dealing

Where do we go from here? What do I do
with these feelings? Longing to have you
near, knowing we shouldn't be dealing . . .
                                   ~Eric Roberson

"How in hell are you going to change the locks
on a house I paid for?" Sean hollered into the
phone. I was at the shop, making my money, but
I'd taken the liberty of calling a locksmith while
he was gone. It didn't make a difference to me if
Mother Nature had paid for that house. I didn't
want him in there until I could figure out what
I was going to do. Now, I might have felt differently had he called while he was gone to rectify
the situation, but if he thought that he was going
to screw in my bed and slide right back through
like nothing had happened, he was bugging.

"Get Carla to assist you in finding a place to
stay until I figure things out. I can't deal with
this right now," I responded, throwing his line
back at him.

"You can't deal with what? Are you serious?" he continued to yell as I excused myself from my client to finish the call. I ran a very professional shop, and when dealing with a client, that was their time. I didn't allow my stylists to hold phone conversations while working, and I firmly believed in leading by example.

"Excuse me, Ms. Waters. This call will be very short," I told my client as I stepped away from my station and took the call out front. Just in case I had to say a few choice words, I didn't want to be in earshot of the clientele. I didn't need them thinking I had any issues that would affect the shop.

"Valencia, you are really taking this to another level," Sean said, continuing to rant and rave.

I was getting a headache just talking to him. "Your bare dick in your assistant in our bed is what took it to another level, Sean. You had sex in our bed! What part of that is going over your head? There's no use in staying at the house, because I have a full book today and I'll be here late. I've changed the locks and the alarm settings, and I would hate for you to get locked up for breaking and entering," I explained to him as calmly as possible. I wanted to wild the hell out, but I had the entire shop's eyes on me even through the glass window and I had to hold it together.

"Would it have been better if we had sex at a hotel? You're taking this shit somewhere else, and you're really pissing me off. You are the one that got fat as hell. You didn't hold up your end of the bargain."

"My end of the bargain?"

"Yeah, your end of the bargain. If I wanted to marry an elephant, I could have gotten one a lot cheaper at the zoo."

I had to hold the phone away from my face and look at it to make sure I wasn't trippin'. This fool must have bumped his head. "Well, my fat ass is at the shop, making my money, so figure it out."

"Valencia, you have to be—"

"I'm not kidding, Sean," I said, cutting him off mid-sentence. "Besides, I got rid of everything in the bedroom, so there is nowhere for you to lie."

"You did what!" he exclaimed in disbelief. "So what do you want me to do?"

"Go to hell," I said in a measured tone. "But for now, try finding a room at the Four Seasons," I retorted, borrowing a line from Beyoncé in the movie *Obsessed*, then straight banged on his ass. I didn't have time for the shenanigans with him today. That last statement cut deep, but I wouldn't give Sean the satisfaction of thinking he had me defeated. Today he would not win.

Heading back into the shop, I attempted to pick up where I left off, not wanting the nonsense with Sean to ruin the rest of my day. I had a lot of time to think while he was away, and although I wasn't convinced that I was heading toward divorce, I knew that if I didn't straighten this mess up quickly, it would be more of the same from him down the line. I didn't care if I put on a million pounds. You didn't shit where you ate. I didn't have to know that they were seeing each other, but that just went to show that men couldn't never do shit right. It wasn't always like this, and I wondered briefly if it ever could be back the way it was.

The night we went dancing played in my head like it had just happened the other day. I decided after the fifth bouquet of flowers arrived that week that I would call this man and tell him I would go dancing with him. I was actually kind of excited, because I'd never been salsa dancing before, and from what everyone said, it was an easy dance to pick up.

I had my team do the damn thing to me as usual, and I found a sexy little red dress perfect for doing the salsa. It was form fitting, was low cut on the top, belled out toward the bottom, had a peekaboo slit on the side, and stopped just below the knee. I was very pleased with my look when I was done, and found the perfect red stiletto from the Fergie line to match. I was the official lady in red.

Sean had me picked up at the shop in a custom-made Bentley Continental GTZ, which even had my mouth open when it pulled up. I had him pick me up from the shop because I was working late and wouldn't have time to go all the way home. Plus, it was easier to take a shower in the back and stay in my bathrobe while my hair and everything got done. That way everything would be perfect, and I could walk right out. I also wasn't sure I wanted him to know where I lived just yet, just in case he had stalker tendencies.

Terrell, forever the fairy godmother, fluffed my hair out once more before walking me to the car. The driver was very handsome and patiently waited for me to get adjusted in the backseat before closing the door and trotting around to the other side. I rolled down the window to wave good-bye to my friends as we drove off into the unknown. Jersey wasn't that far away, so I figured I'd take a small sip of the complimentary bubbly that was provided as I sat back and enjoyed the ride. I couldn't really see out of the tinted windows, but I had my cell phone on full charge so that once I got where I needed to be, I could text my friends and close family the address of where I would be.

I wasn't sure how far we drove, but I was in shock for the second time that night. Instead of pulling up to a swank nightclub, we parked on a landing strip, in front of a jet. The driver extended his hand to help me out, and he held my hand all the way over to the jet, even helping me up the steps. When I got inside, I saw it was decked out! A nice gold and burgundy decor ran throughout. From the plush carpeting to the window treatments, this joint was laid. I never thought I would be this up close and personal to something so fly, since I'd seen this type of stuff only on *MTV Cribs*. Sean was seated comfortably, sipping red wine from a gold-rimmed glass, and damn, was he looking good. I was suddenly glad I at least wore a thong to sop up some of the juices.

"Glad you could join me, Miss Lady," Sean greeted me after setting his glass down and taking my hand from the chauffeur's to usher me farther into the jet's cabin. I was still speechless and couldn't believe my luck. Had I really just hit the jackpot?

"Wow, all of this to go to Jersey?" I asked in awe as I took my seat. A giddy laugh escaped my lips, and I tried to control my rapidly beating heart. I had never flown in a jet before, and my nerves were getting the best of me. The door closed, and I could hear the pilot getting ready for liftoff.

"Well, there has been a slight change of plans," Sean said as he got comfortable in the seat next to me.

"Are we still going dancing?" I asked with wide eyes. It ran across my mind for a quick second that this man was going to take me to a secret bat cave and tie me to a bed in a dungeon, making me his sex slave, but I quickly dismissed the thought . . . kind of.

"Yeah, we're still going dancing, and I'm ready to salsa all night." He smiled at me, doing a quick two-step in his seat, which made me laugh. I could feel myself calming down.

"Okay, so where are we going?"

"To the salsa nation," he responded after buckling his seat belt. "Although they aren't the originators, it's damn close. Besides, travel to Cuba is restricted."

"Okay." I smiled at him, following suit and buckling my seat belt. "Where to?"

"Puerto Rico."

I Can Do Bad All by Myself

*I don't need no one to put me down. I'm on
the ground, can't get no lower. And I don't
need no one to hang around and make me
frown, just makes me look older. . . .*
                                        ~Mary J Blige

When I got home, I was relieved to see that
Sean's car wasn't parked in the driveway, but
I was kind of hoping it would be. In my head
it would mean that he at least cared enough to
wait for me. I tried not to let me mind wander,
but I figured he was probably laid up with his assistant some damn where. I swear, I hated them
both. How could he do this to me?

Standing in front of the mirror in the guest
room in my bra and panties, I took a good long
look at myself. Where there used to be a flat
tummy that sported a cute little butterfly tattoo
on my hip bone, there was now a glob of flesh
that hung over my panty line. Once perky breasts

now sat flat on my stomach like dog ears, and my cute little butterfly tattoo was now deformed, out of shape, and tucked under my gut. Damn, this shit was depressing.

Making my way to the kitchen, I took out two single-serve containers of my favorite ice cream, Turkey Hill butter pecan, afterward thinking better of it and putting one back. Grabbing a spoon, I took a seat at the counter and began to ponder where we went wrong and at what point it all started.

I remembered the dance like it was yesterday. I was still in awe as we jetted across the globe and landed in San Juan, Puerto Rico. The weather was a steamy ninety degrees, which felt wonderful against my skin. I definitely looked the part as we exited the jet on a landing strip and ran to safety. Sean complimented my hair, which was swept to the side, with curls cascading down past my shoulders. Miami Glow by J Lo radiated from my skin in waves and wrapped around us as we walked down to the waiting Aston Martin, which would be taking us to the club. Sean's Boss Pure by Hugo Boss tickled my nose in the warm night breeze as we sat cuddled up in the car. I assured him that I was just fine, but that I needed to let my friends know I had arrived safely.

We pulled up to the Nuyorican Café, where a live band was in full swing and the dance floor was packed. The energy in the room already had me moving my feet, and I was ready to get the party started. Sean did not hesitate to sweep me up and drag me on the dance floor, where we stayed for the remainder of the evening. San Juan was gorgeous, and the people were really friendly. We shared at least three *mojitos* in between sets as the band took breaks, and I was really enjoying myself.

The night got even better when we did as the other visitors did and club hopped down the strip. We even took a break and ate a scrumptious meal at one of the outdoor bar and grills on our way down. Any food we ate was danced off immediately, and I was having the time of my life. At around six in the morning, we found ourselves strolling hand in hand on the beach, Sean carrying both of our shoes in a little knapsack we found along the way.

The ocean water felt warm as it rushed past us, covering our feet up to our ankles, before sliding back out in gentle waves. Along the way we came across a set of huge boulders, which we climbed up on. I sat between his legs, with my head leaned back into the crook of his neck, as he held me in a tight embrace. We chatted about everything as the sun came up and blessed us with its presence. I wondered briefly if Sean would be the right man for me, but then decided to just enjoy the ride to see where it would go.

On our way back to the car we held hands, and I felt so safe with Sean. I hadn't felt like this in a good long minute, and especially not with my ex. He was too stuck on himself to give me this kind of attention, and when it was finally over, I was happy. Sean oozed confidence, but not in a cocky way. He appeared to be a take-charge kind of man and seemed sure about what he wanted. It took a special kind of person to be able to juggle and be responsible for everyone's finances and not mess it up. That showed me that he was about business first.

We pulled into a cute little bed-and-breakfast not too far from the beach. What struck me as odd—but I kind of liked it—was when we were seated for breakfast, instead of sitting across from me, Sean pulled our chairs next to each other. He casually draped his arm across my shoulders, and we fed each other strawberries and talked about our night. My phone had died a long time ago, and I knew Terrell had called at least a million times. When I told him we were salsa dancing in Puerto Rico, he'd gone clean off.

"It's officially Sunday morning, princess," Sean said into my ear as we picked over breakfast. Both of us were exhausted from partying like rock stars all night, and I personally was ready for a nap. "Let's say we see if they have any available space in this establishment, and we'll crash for a minute before heading back home. How does that sound?"

"Lead the way," I responded in the middle of a yawn as I grabbed my shoes. I enjoyed the view as Sean walked ahead of me, and I couldn't believe how my weekend was turning out.

Now, this was the true test for myself. We were about to be alone in a hotel room, and to be honest with myself, Sean turned me on. He was moving on the dance floor, so I knew he had a serious rhythm going on. Would it transfer to the bedroom? Was I even ready for that? This was a delicate line we were about to cross. If I slept with him too soon, that would knock my potential "wifey" status down to merely being a quickie, one-night chick. At the same time we were both grown, so why not?

I had a million butterflies in my stomach as we waited for our suite to be cleaned. The desk clerk apologized for the delay, and since they didn't have a room ready, they kind of pushed the couple that was in there along to accommodate us.

We just had to wait for housekeeping to finish. A man with power turned me on even more. This was going to be hard.

Fifteen minutes later we were escorted up to our suite by the staff. A covered tray was pushed behind us as we walked, and Sean held my hand the entire time. When we got into the suite, it was breathtaking. It faced the ocean, and I loved the Southern feel it had. On the bed there was a silk chemise lying next to a pair of silk pajama pants, which I assumed were for Sean.

After tipping the bellhop, Sean closed the door behind him and began removing his jewelry, laying it next to our cell phones, which were both dead. It was foolish of me to leave my charger at home, but for some reason I felt safe with him, so I didn't worry. He took the food from the tray and spread it out on the counter in the kitchen area. He turned the TV on while I took a shower.

After pinning my hair up and sliding on a shower cap, I exhaled as the steam surrounded me and the extra hot water beat down on my tired body. I didn't realize how tired I actually was until the water hit me. Taking the coconut and banana shower gel, courtesy of the hotel, from the ledge, I worked up a nice lather all over my body and quickly rinsed off so that I could do it again.

This time around, I took my time and pretended my fingertips were his as I traced the outline of my nipples and allowed my hand to reach down to where my legs formed a V. Using my fingers to spread my lips, I used my middle finger to stir up the pot, sliding back up to trace small circles on my clit. Suppressing a moan, I leaned against the tile wall of the shower so that I wouldn't slip and fall as my body began to convulse from a quickly approaching orgasm. I had to hold on to the glass sliding door for support because my legs were getting weak.

After rinsing off for the last time and getting myself together, I stepped out and wrapped one of the fluffy towels around my body, snatching the shower cap from my head and brushing my hair, which was still a little curly, even after the shower, up into a cute side ponytail. Looking around, I realized I'd forgotten to take my chemise from the bed, so I really had no choice but to go out with the towel on. Looking in the mirror, I noticed the towel barely covered my ass, but what could I do? Tucking it extra tight between my breasts, I snatched the coconut-banana lotion from the counter and proceeded out of the bathroom. I'd just have to make sure the towel stayed on.

Upon coming out of the bathroom, I found Sean fast asleep on the bed. I must have taken longer than I thought I had in the shower. He looked so cute lying there with his shirt pulled from his slacks, showing a Gucci belt buckle. I couldn't help but imagine looking at him every morning forever. Grabbing the chemise from the bed, I doubled back to the bathroom and slipped into it, minus panties, because I didn't have any with me. After properly moisturizing my skin and applying a little gloss to my lips, I went out to wake Sean up.

Tiptoeing across the floor, I leaned over Sean to get a good look at him. He had the most gorgeous eyelashes I'd ever seen, and I loved that he kept a well-groomed situation. His lineup looked fresh, and he might have gotten his eyebrows arched. He had nice full lips, but not overly done. They looked kissable. I had to make myself back up before I undid his pants and had my way with him.

"Sean," I called out as I shook him lightly. "Sean, I'm out of the shower now. Sorry I took so long."

He opened his eyes and stretched his body. Damn, he even looked good just waking up. Stepping back, I gave him room to sit up and took the liberty of helping him remove his shirt.

He wasn't overly muscular, but you could tell he definitely worked out. It wasn't like I could use his abs to count to six or anything, but he was nice to look at.

"I'm sorry, princess. I didn't realize how tired I was," he said in a groggy voice. "I'm glad I got the right size for you. I wanted it to be a surprise."

"Fits perfectly," I responded, doing a little circle to show him the entire outfit. "Now, let's get you in the shower. I'm a little exhausted myself."

Taking a seat on the other side of the bed, I watched him as he walked into the bathroom to shower. I couldn't see him getting undressed, but once he got into the shower, I could almost see his outline through the glass door from my spot in the bed. My hands almost found their way back down south, but I refrained, instead turning and putting my hands under the pillow.

My plan was to wait for him to get out of the shower, but I must have fallen asleep. I didn't realize it until I felt him get in the bed and wrap himself around me. It was like a natural fit as I scooted back some so that we could spoon. A small part of me hoped he would reach down and see I didn't have on any underwear, but I was kind of glad he didn't. I didn't want this, whatever "this" was, to just turn into a sex thing between us. It would be nice to see if we could build something.

Both Sean and I slept well into the afternoon, and it felt great to have a warm body next to me again. It'd been ages since I'd had the company of a man, and that was totally by choice. I had to take the time I needed to get me together, and I didn't want to go into the next relationship with baggage from the last one. I needed to heal, and I needed to feel free again.

As I snuggled up with Sean, I felt like I was ready to live that kind of life again. The me I was then was the best I had to offer, and I was going in with my eyes wide open. I would slow walk this one, and if it was meant to be, it would be. Keeping it real, I'd say that I was tempted to get things popping when I felt his erection pressing against the crack of my ass, but I wouldn't make the first move. We'd have plenty of time for that, and if it was meant to happen, then happen it would.

When It Hurts

So before we get into the things that we shouldn't do, I'ma need your undivided attention. 'Cause it's fantasies and reality. Baby, which one are we living in . . .

~Avant

"Why won't you accept my calls? Why do you keep ignoring my text messages? Valencia, you are really taking all of this to the extreme." Sean's voice came over my answering machine for the millionth time in the last few days. All he could do was call the house, because I changed my cell phone number, and little did he know the house phone was next. The only reason why I hadn't changed the number at the shop was that it was business, and I wasn't about to let him mess that up. Besides that, he could just go there, so there was no hiding from him.

"Listen, when you're ready to grow up, you know how to contact me. I'm not stooping down to your level. If I was you, I'd act fast, because I don't know how long I will wait," he concluded after leaving ten more messages like the previous one.

Sean was trying to throw his weight around. Not that it mattered, because him leaving wasn't something I had a choice in. We had been growing apart for years, and it wasn't just about the weight thing. I wasn't sure if I even wanted to stick around my damn self. It had started as a night away from home here and there, which he tried to pass off as business. Those turned into weekends away, and flicks of him with other chicks, laid up on exotic beaches, popping up on the Net. He tried to convince me that they were Photoshopped pics, but I never believed him.

Now, with a man like Sean, and the status he had, there was bound to be a hoochie in the tuck, trying to take him from me. That was one of the laws of physics. Especially since we didn't really get a chance to know each other before we jumped the broom. I mean, we knew each other, but not as well as we should have for us to want to exchange vows. We weren't exactly on some Biggie and Faith–type stuff, but it happened pretty quickly.

We ended up staying at the hotel in Puerto Rico until the next morning, and I managed to find a pair of panties along the way. After catching up on sleep, which lasted until the late afternoon, we took in the sites of San Juan before having dinner at La Cucina di Ivo, where Sean knew the owner, Ivo Bignami. The meal was delicious. Afterward, we managed to sleep the entire night without doing anything more than cuddling.

Early the next morning we chartered the same jet back home. On board we enjoyed a nice breakfast and were able to sit back and relax. No one could have told me that I would be salsa dancing and spending the weekend in San Juan with one of the most sought-after men on the planet. My luck was never that good! When we finally made it back to the airport here in Philly, a car was there to take us home, and Sean made sure I got all the way to the door. He was very respectful, and we shared a hug and a quick peck on the lips before he was off, promising to contact me before the week was out.

This man had me floating on cloud nine, and even during my nap I could feel myself smiling in my sleep. I plugged my phone in but left it off because I knew Terrell and everyone else had been blowing me up and I wasn't really ready to come down off my high just yet. I couldn't wait to tell everyone about my weekend, but it could wait until tomorrow. For now, I had to reorder permanent and semipermanent colors, contact the rep that supplied my relaxer line because they had messed up on my last order, and pick up a few odds and ends from the local hair store, like plastic caps and wrap strips. I hated to run out of things, and for that reason my shop was always well stocked. My shop didn't open on Mondays, but that didn't exactly mean a day off for me.

"Diva, give us the juice!" I heard from the back of the shop on Tuesday morning, before I even saw Terrell's face. He brought so much energy to the place—even at that early morning hour.

"Well, let's just say the Puerto Ricans know how to move! We were dancing all over that island." I smiled as I recapped the past weekend.

"I thought y'all were going to Jersey," Terrell inquired as we unpacked the bags I brought in, and put everything in its proper place. I already had two clients waiting, so I could give him only a tidbit for now.

"I thought the same thing, but since when did we have to charter a jet to go across the bridge?" I playfully spilled the beans, dragging him along.

"Oh, I am so open right now!" Terrell responded with exaggerated flare, like only he could, drawing a round of laughs from everyone in attendance.

Shaking my head, I made my way to the front to start on my first client.

Things with Sean and me progressed at a fast pace. We spent the very next Sunday on the beach in Belize, where I was mesmerized by the pink sand. We managed to sneak in a few Broadway shows over the space of a month, and we even snuck in a few shopping sprees where the sky was the limit. Honestly, he had to force me to buy something, because I wasn't into getting things from men I'd just met. I didn't want him thinking he was going to treat me like a groupie because he'd dropped a couple thousand on a Chanel bag. There was nothing he could buy me that I couldn't get myself, and I had to make that perfectly clear before finally letting him purchase a bag and a pair of sandals to match from Michael Kors. I could have gone with Gucci, but I figured we'd start with something that didn't cost as much and take it from there.

Pretty soon we were in it like six months deep, and although Sean was constantly moving and shaking, I loved how he made time for me. We had some serious talks along the way, and I was glad I didn't have to remind him that the way to keep me around was to keep doing the things that he did in the beginning. I wasn't a fool, though, and I knew that there would be moments when he couldn't get away; that just kind of came with the business. Hell, I owned a salon that was growing by the day, so that meant I wouldn't always be able to fly to Africa at the drop of a hat as well. We were very respectful of each other's time, and that was really what kept us going.

I liked Sean. Okay, I really liked him, and I would almost go as far as saying I loved him, but not all the way. Just the thought of him put butterflies in my stomach and made me smile at the oddest moments. I could be out grocery shopping, and something he might have said a week or so ago would pop in my head and make me smile. Or I could be watching a show and might see something funny that was reminiscent of him, and I would be cracking up at it. Sean made me happy, but did that constitute love? I wasn't in a rush to tie the knot, and I wanted to be sure that he was the one. I'd vowed to get married only one time in my life, and if he was the one, we were in it to the very end.

I was excited on one particular day, because it had been about two weeks since I had seen Sean, and we hadn't really got to talk that much. He was in Switzerland, handling business for a few accounts he had over there for himself as well as for some clients, and he told me before he left that because of the way the meetings were set up and the time difference, he wouldn't be able to talk to me a whole lot. I missed him and was glad that he was able to make time a few nights and call after he was done. It would be like three in the morning when my phone rang, but I would wake right up and talk to him.

I couldn't wait to see Sean, and curiosity had my stomach in knots the entire day. He told me he had a surprise for me, and my only instructions were to dress in all black and be ready by eight, because he would be sending a car to pick me up. I was ready by seven and was pacing back and forth in my living room, waiting for the car to show up. I was curious as to what might happen. Were we jet setting to another exotic island? Were we going shopping? Or maybe out dancing? It didn't really matter to me what was happening. As long as I was with him, I was happy.

The car arrived a few minutes early, and I was out the door and in the backseat in no time. I was feeling giddy and excited, and was smiling so hard, my cheeks were hurting. I couldn't wait to see Sean, and I felt like a little kid in the backseat with my face pushed up to the glass, trying to see out of the tinted windows. I couldn't really tell where we were going, and I tried to read the signs, but the car was moving too fast and everything was a blur. Sitting back in the seat, I decided it would be best to just calm down and let the night flow effortlessly.

Not too long after, the car pulled up to what looked like a castle. The driver helped me out of the car, and I had to hold his hand for a few more seconds to get my balance and close my mouth. Was this Sean's place? I mean, I knew he was rolling in the dough, but damn. I didn't even get a chance to take in the surroundings from the circular driveway before I was ushered into the house.

The foyer was breathtaking. I almost didn't even want to walk across the marble floors, as my heels clicked against them on my way to the dining room. The floor-to-ceiling windows were heavily draped with cream and burgundy curtains, probably made from some imported Italian silk or something like that. Delicious smells wafted from the back of the house, and my stomach growled a little bit in anticipation of the meal. I was escorted past the dining room and right into the gourmet kitchen, where I found Sean at the stove centered in an island, doing his thing.

"So you're a gourmet chef as well? Lucky me."
I smiled as I took the apron he offered me and
tied it around my waist. Sweeping my hair to the
side, I took the liberty of coming out of my heels
and stepping into the flats Sean had laid out for
me.

"Princess, I'm a man of many talents," Sean
responded as he tended to a bubbling pot of red
sauce that I couldn't wait to taste. "Let me bor-
row your tongue for a minute."

The look on my face spoke volumes, but I
sidled up right next to him and waited. As he
stirred the pot, he leaned into me and kissed my
lips. Setting the spoon down, he was able to turn
toward me, and I stepped right into his arms. He
wrapped his muscular arms around me and held
me close. Teasing the corners of his lips with the
tip of my tongue, I took the liberty of memoriz-
ing the shape of his mouth and let his tongue ex-
plore mine. Damn, I wanted to make love to this
man, and if I had it my way, tonight would be the
night. Breaking from the kiss, Sean continued to
hold me close as he swiped the spoon around the
pot once more, and after blowing it cool, he held
the spoon up to my lips to taste the sauce.

"How does that taste, princess?" Sean asked
after kissing me again.

"It's delicious," I responded, gathering the sauce from the corner of my mouth with my fingertip, then sticking my finger into his mouth to clean it.

"That's just the beginning. I have a scrumptious meal planned for us, followed by dessert that's to die for. Are you ready for a night of relaxation?"

Instead of answering, I kissed him again, and in the back of my mind I knew tonight would be the night. I wondered if Sean would always be this attentive, but then remembered to rein in my feelings. This was supposed to be a fun thing . . . right? Sitting at the small table that was set for us on the other side of the island, I waited for Sean to join me, and as he served our meal, we talked about our future. I wasn't sure if this was going to be a forever thing, but we were definitely off to a great start.

Who Knows

Who knows somehow this night just might lead us into a place where our emotions can grow if we let them go. . . .
                                    ~Musiq Soulchild

"Valencia, you can either come outside and we'll talk like adults, or I'll just come in there and we can talk in front of the entire shop. Either way, we're going to talk today. You have a minute to decide how you want to handle this."

"Sean, I'm handling business right now, and I have clients that need to be serviced. We can talk later today, when I get home."

"That's not an option, and you know how I hate repeating myself. Either come out or I'm coming in. Your call."

Sean had been on my heels for about two weeks now. Ever since I caught him long stroking his assistant, I hadn't really had too much to say to him. I knew I had to eventually deal with the situation, but I just didn't feel like picking up the pieces at the present moment. He assured me that she'd been fired and all that, but he might have been better off keeping her around. It would be a cold day in hell before he lay down in bed with me again.

I had yet to move back into our bedroom, even with the new bed and bedroom decor. It was like an entirely new room, and I made sure he paid for everything that went in there. I even took our wedding photo down, because it didn't seem like that was going to be a part of our reality for too much longer. Besides that, it had a bullet hole in it, and I didn't want to be reminded of that horrible day. I guess he figured if he gave me his black card, he could get back in. Silly him. I used that card until the stripe on the back was gone, and he still wasn't getting a key. I took our marriage vows very seriously, and the sad part was we might be actually talking divorce.

"Sean, let me finish curling Mrs. Gray and I'll be out. Give me fifteen minutes."

I straight banged on his ass without waiting for a reply. I didn't feel like dealing with this mess with Sean today. I wasn't exactly having the best day, after all; I woke up with a splitting headache and had been running behind ever since. I was already an hour behind when I locked my keys and everything in the car at the gas station, and it took forever for AAA to come and let me in, and my car was running the entire time. I could see my phone ringing inside my car, and between Sean and Terrell, I didn't know who to call first. The cashier was kind enough to allow me to use the phone to call for assistance and to let Terrell know I was running late. I didn't want to push the envelope and make another call just to argue with my cheating-ass husband. He could wait. I just needed to get to the shop so that I could get started.

By the time I pulled up, my first three clients were, thankfully, still under the dryer or in some stage of getting prepped, and I walked in with two more on my heels. This was definitely going to be a busy day. I had yet to call Sean back, and on the real I probably wouldn't. I didn't feel like his shit right now, and he already knew I didn't discuss my personal business at my place of business. I would just have to catch up with him whenever.

I was finally getting back into the grove of things when this fool decided to show up. Why wasn't he at the office, making power moves, or overseas with one of the many hoochies that he obviously had? I knew he had some other shit to do besides ride my ass all day, but Sean was stubborn and would not leave until he got his way. I didn't feel like this shit today.

Giving Terrell the heads-up, I stepped outside to talk to Sean. I felt bad rushing through my client's hairstyle, but I just needed to get Sean off my back so that I could get through the rest of my day. I didn't need this to drag out any more than it already had, but this was not the kind of situation that was resolved with a snappy decision. I had to decide what I was going to do with the rest of my life, and I didn't know if that included him.

"Sean, can we please make this quick? I have a full book today, and I really don't have the energy to go through it with you right now."

He wanted me to have a seat in his car so that we could talk, but I refused to get in. If I was standing outside, at least I could walk away when I was ready. He put up a fuss for a while, but once he realized I wasn't going to budge, he just went on with what he had to say. While he was talking, I couldn't help but wonder where we went wrong. What happened to the man I fell in love with and married? Was weight gain really the root of all the bullshit that was going on? I was in a daze while he was talking, wondering what moves I needed to make next.

Sean and I were definitely in love, and the night he proposed to me always brought tears to my eyes when I thought about it. We were out one night, slumming it at the Cheesecake Factory after catching a flick at the Loews theater in Cherry Hill. It was a warm summer night, so we took seats out on the deck, where we could eat by candlelight and talk without having to yell over the hustle and bustle of the restaurant. It was a more intimate setting, and I appreciated the privacy.

We were holding hands across the table after the waitress took our order, and as we discussed what we would be doing that week, Sean's facial expression changed. He looked serious only when he had something he needed to say and didn't quite know how. It had me concerned for a minute, and when I asked him if he was okay, he assured me he was. I didn't believe him.

"Sean, you seem distracted," I said to him as we neared the end of our meal. We'd had a pretty decent conversation, but I could tell his mind was elsewhere.

"You know, I feel like sometimes people spend too much time procrastinating on things that need to be handled immediately, and the things that can wait, they rush out to do," he said with a straight face, which was the exact opposite of the confusion written all over mine.

"Ummm . . . okay. I guess you have a point there," was my response. I didn't really know what to say. I didn't want him to think I wasn't following his line of thought, but truth be told, I didn't know where he was going with it.

"Valencia, how long have we been dating?"

"I want to say a little over four months," I responded carefully as I quickly calculated the days in my head.

"And how long have you been loving me?"

I paused, looking him in the eye. Where was he going with this? I had yet to reveal to Sean that I actually loved him, although I did make sure that he knew I did care. Was he saying he loved me and wanted to make things official? Okay, I had to get my thoughts together. Did I really want a relationship with him? We had yet to make love. What if it was wack? So many thoughts went through my mind, and I couldn't even speak. I didn't want to make a fool out of myself.

"For a while," I responded, deciding to just keep it real with him. What did I have to lose? I did love him. I loved being around him, I loved talking to him, and I missed him when he was gone . . . all of the above. I'd fantasized about being his wife, but we just met and were still getting to know each other, so I didn't allow my thoughts to consume me. Sean never pressured me into anything, and I respected him for that. That was one of the things I loved about him, but now he had me wondering.

"I loved you the first night I saw you at that party. Out of all the people in the room, I knew you were something special." He smiled as he talked to me. I, on the other hand, was at a loss for words. "There was something in your eyes that drew me in. Even in the midst of having fun, you were about your business. I like that in a woman."

"Wow," I said, trying to keep my tears in check. Sean had caught me completely off guard. "I don't know what to say."

"Say you'll marry me."

It was like time stood still for a second and then began to move in slow motion. I could see his lips moving, but I couldn't hear what he was saying. I watched him through blurred vision as he got up from his seat. I could see violinists coming out from behind him, and although they were playing music, I couldn't hear it. I just saw their arms moving back and forth. I watched him get down on one knee next to me and pull an Emma Parker box from his top pocket. I watched in stunned silence as he pulled the top back and the most gorgeous ring I'd ever seen winked at me from a satin setting. Was this man proposing to me for real?

"Valencia, I've spent most of my life looking for the perfect fit in this imperfect world. I'm willing to except you, flaws and all, because I come with flaws, too. I feel like you compliment me, because I come to you already complete and happy. I'm ready to spend the rest of my life with one person, and I see everything I'm looking for in you. Will you please do me the honor of accepting my proposal? Will you make me the happiest man in the world and marry me?"

It was like it was only he and I left on the planet. I couldn't see or hear anything else. This man wanted to marry me? Me! Out of all the beautiful women in the world, whom I was sure he had the pick of, he wanted me. Was I dreaming?

"Yes, Sean," I said through my tears, "I'll marry you."

I wasn't even aware that a crowd had formed around us, until he slid the ring on my finger and I heard the applause. Sean picked me up from the chair and held me in his arms as we kissed. My tears wouldn't stop flowing, and Sean couldn't stop smiling. As the violinist kicked the music up into high gear, we sat and enjoyed our dessert as folks walked past and congratulated us.

"Listen, pull out a couple of bottles of your best champagne and give everyone in the restaurant a glass. It's time for a toast," Sean told our waitress as we gathered our stuff up to go. I was smiling so hard, my cheeks hurt, and I couldn't wait to get on the horn and tell everyone what had happened. As we stood in front of the restaurant and waited for everyone to get a glass in their hand, Sean continued to look into my eyes. I could see the love in his, and I had a great feeling about this. This thing was going to last a lifetime.

"Does everyone have a glass in their hand?" Sean asked as the room became quiet.

Everyone held up their glass in response.

"Good. I'm happy to be here in this moment, and I just wanted to take a minute to show all of you the wonderful woman I have. I'm going to give her the world," he said, his voice cracking a little as a tear threatened to fall from his pretty hazel eyes. "I'm really the lucky one, and if you have a person in your life that makes you feel that way, don't wait any longer to let them know. Valencia, I love you, and I know this is going to last forever." He ended the speech with a kiss, and the applause was almost deafening as the crowd went wild. Sean instructed the waitress to serve the bottles of champagne until they were empty, and after the bill was paid, we headed out.

Now, I'd been to Sean's house only once, and that was for dinner. He was a respectable man, so after a tour of the place, we sat by the fireplace, where we fed each other chocolate-covered strawberries and sipped some wine until it got late. We moved our party to a beautiful chaise lounge that was wide enough to hold us both, and we just talked until the wee hours of the morning as we spooned, with me in the front.

The night he proposed, I had a feeling that more than just spooning was going to take place, and I was definitely ready to take it there. I'd been a good girl for a while, so it was time to show Sean what he would be working with. As we made our way back to his house, I held his hand as he controlled the wheel with his other. I couldn't stop staring at my ring. The diamond halo setting in white gold looked wonderful against the two-carats that sat in the middle. Sean had definitely outdone himself. As we pulled up to his mansion, I prepared myself mentally. It was about to go down, and tonight would be a night Sean would never forget.

My Love

You chose her 'cause she's sweet as pie.
Take what you give, even your lies. But,
baby, are you happy without me?
                                        ~Jill Scott

"I think maybe we should see a marriage counselor. We've both invested too much not to try and make things work."

To appease Sean, I decided to meet him for dinner at Phillips Seafood in the Sheraton Hotel in downtown Philly. It was convenient because that was where, he claimed, he was staying since I locked him out of the house. I figured once we were done dinner, he could just carry his ass right up to his room. I don't think Sean realized how painful it was to catch him the way I did, and it wasn't really about making him suffer.

It was more about deciding if I wanted to live a life of mistrust. The dynamics of our relationship changed that day. I couldn't help but wonder if that was his first time having sex outside of the marriage. I know for sure he had been tapping his assistant for some time, but how many others were there? Sean wasn't interested in having sex with me, and hadn't been for months, so he had to be getting it from somewhere. Especially since when we first hooked up, we had sex all the damn time. The bigger situation was that I knew if the tables were turned and I were the one who'd been caught, he'd have hung me out to dry and I'd be back living with my momma, putting my name on the orange juice. I just wasn't willing to go through the nonsense.

"A counselor? And what exactly would we be getting from this 'counseling'? You're a cheater, plain and simple. What more do we have to discuss?"

"Damn it, Valencia! Why are you making this more difficult than it has to be?" Sean barked, slamming his hand down on the table, causing the few people in the restaurant to turn and look at us. How embarrassing was that? I looked at him like he was crazy.

"How am I making you cheating on me more difficult? You're the reason why we're even having this conversation. You were the one that got caught cheating, or did you forget that important factor?"

This man must have bumped his head on the way down here to dinner. I would dare him to try and flip this shit on me like it was my fault. I had tried to approach him to get things popping, and he never wanted to do anything. I knew it was over when I caught myself waking him up with a blow job, and his dick didn't even stir a little bit. That was when I knew for sure it was a wrap on us. Sean had exactly been helpful, either. I knew I was putting on weight, but before I knew it, I was already too fat for him.

"That's not what I'm saying."

"Then, what are you saying, because I'm not beat for this shit?"

Why couldn't we go back to how things used to be? When Sean proposed to me, I was happy as hell. When we got home that night, he set the date, and the very next day he had me out getting things together. I had to find a hall, a dress, call my family. . . . It was so overwhelming, and I found myself going in circles. I ended up at Terrell's house, because I knew that he would make sense of it all.

Terrell was the bomb in every sense of the word. He was like the sister I wished I could have had if I didn't already have a sister. He had a stunning town house near the airport that was, of course, decorated immaculately. He'd missed his calling, definitely, because he would have made a killing being an interior decorator to the stars. He could make colors work that folks wouldn't normally put together. I loved asking him to describe his place to people, because he never mentioned colors. Everything was a food of some type. To me, his living room had dark brown walls, purple furniture, and green accents, but Terrell would quickly check you and let you know that his living room was chocolate, with grape furniture and celery accents. You had to love him.

"Diva! Welcome to my humble abode." My best friend greeted me at the door with air kisses and a tight hug. I instantly felt at ease. "What brings you to my neck of the woods, Ms. Thang?" Terrell asked as I followed him into the kitchen.

Taking a seat at his custom-made breakfast nook, I watched him as he busied himself around the kitchen, getting out a teapot and some scones to snack on. I waited for him to stop moving, and instead of saying a word, I held up my ring finger.

"Diva! He put a ring on it? Girrlll . . ."

"Last night we went out to dinner after I left the shop, and he proposed."

"Do give me all the juicy details! I knew he would be a good catch!" Terrell said excitedly as he examined my new jewelry. I was so giddy with excitement, I didn't know where to begin. The smile on Terrell's face spoke volumes.

"So I had a taste for some cheesecake, and Sean, always eager to please, took me to the Cheesecake Factory for dinner. . . ."

I got into telling Terrell the story, and I couldn't help but laugh as he munched on scones and kept eye contact like I was telling him the latest gossip on the street. His theatrics were comical as he caught his breath and paused at the right moments. The oohs and aahs were hilarious as well, and by the time I summed the story up, he was damn near in tears.

"We walked out hand in hand after he paid the bill, and when we got to his house, which you would have a ball decorating, we just chilled."

"Did you give him some, girl?" Terrell inquired as the sound of the tea kettle forced him to get up.

"Not yet. Sean said he wants to do the right thing and wait until we are married. I just hope he is the truth, because I would hate to marry him and the sex is wack," I joked halfheartedly. Sean was fine as hell, and from what I felt while in Puerto Rico, he was definitely holding on to something lovely, but that didn't mean that he knew what to do with it. I was praying that this man was on point.

"So, diva," Terrell began as if he was in deep thought. He knew me better than anyone, so I knew whatever he was about to ask me was out of genuine concern. "Do you love him?"

I took a minute to answer, because I'd never kept it less than real with Terrell. Besides, I had to keep it real with myself. Did I love Sean? I'd say yes, but I didn't think that I was in love with him. Could I grow to be in love with him? That was to be determined. Spinning this around in my head a couple times, I was finally able to come up with an answer.

"Yes, I love him."

"Good for you. Now, what colors are we wearing? Because I got to put me a tux on special order ASAP."

Terrell and I talked for the rest of the day as I called my friends and family to tell them the good news. He agreed to help me with whatever I needed for the wedding and to get my girls together. Terrell had great taste, so I knew having him coordinate the wedding would be a good move.

At the shop everyone was ready to get the bachelorette party popping immediately. I was all smiles as the crew, as well as clients, congratulated me and asked about the wedding date. Sean gave me three months to plan the wedding, so I had to move fast. I was cool with that, because the time frame put our wedding in the fall, and I could get tiger lilies for the girls' bouquets. I planned to go with a "falling in love" theme to match the season, and Terrell was extra hype already thinking about how things should look.

The shop was popping for it to be Tuesday, but I wasn't mad about it. I had my eye on the Nissan Murano, so I was busy stacking my chips. I also wanted to add another massage section to the back of the shop, and I needed things to be right. Of course, Sean offered to buy me a new truck, but I wouldn't let him do it. Not that I didn't welcome the help, but I needed him to know I was independent and didn't need him for everything. I wasn't a gold digger by any means and could hold my own.

I finally got a break in the afternoon, so I took the opportunity to sit down and call my mom. She was going to be so happy for me, but I was still a little hesitant because Sean and I hadn't been dating for that long and she might just have a problem with that. I wanted a marriage like hers and my dad's, which would last forever. My parents were going on thirty years of marriage, so I knew it was attainable. I just hoped I found the right man to attain it with.

"Praise the Lord," my mother answered in her always cheerful tone, which made me smile instantly. I hadn't seen my parents in a while, and I figured a trip to Maryland was in order. I initially wanted to tell her over the phone about the engagement, but in person would be even better.

"Hi, Mom," I said into the phone through my smile.

"Hey, baby. How are you? How's business?"

Speaking to my mom always made my heart feel good. She'd been very supportive of me wanting to stay in Philly when they decided they were going to retire in another city. My dad wanted to take it way down south to Florida, but my mother didn't want to be that far away from her children. I had two sisters and a brother, and we were all Momma's babies.

I updated my mom on the goings-on at the shop and in my life, and I took the opportunity to tell her about Sean, because I didn't want it to be a total surprise once I told her about the engagement. She inquired about my siblings as well, and I gave her the information that I knew. My brother was still a ladies' man, although he was doing wonderfully in his classes at Temple University, where he was going for his MBA in sports medicine, and my sisters were both doing great in their respective careers.

"So, what is your schedule looking like at the end of the week? I want to catch up with you and Pop over dinner," I said as I finished up my lunch. I saw my next client walking toward my station, so I knew I had to wrap this conversation up quickly.

"I'm free after church, and I'll ask your father to make sure he doesn't have any meetings with the Masons lined up after church. Is everything okay?" she asked with a little worry in her voice, which I put to rest immediately.

"Mom, everything in my world is perfect right now. I want you to meet somebody, so I'll check his schedule as well and I'll get back to you with a time. We may not be able to make the service, but I think lunch after church is doable."

"You're not pregnant, are you? Lord, what will I tell your father?"

"No, Mom," I responded through my laugh. She tended to forget that I was way old enough to have babies, but if she didn't worry, it wouldn't be her. "I'm not pregnant yet, but things are looking up. I have a client, so I have to go, but I'll see you on Sunday. I love you."

"I love you, too, baby. I'll let your dad know you are coming, and we'll talk again later in the week to confirm."

We said our good-byes, and I hung up with a smile on my face. Rubbing my belly, I wondered how it would feel to be carrying Sean's child. Would we be good parents? Shaking the thought from my head, I got up to clean my area and then tend to my client. I had so much to do in so little time, and I wanted everything to be perfect and to Sean's liking, as well. He'd told me that whatever I wanted would be fine with him, but I wanted him to be included in the decision making. We had to get everyone together, and I had yet to meet any of his friends. I was already feeling light-headed just thinking about it all, but I was ready. In a matter of months I would be Mrs. Sean King, and I would be wearing the title of his "queen" well.

Please Return My Call

*It's been too long since I've seen your face
. . . since I've smelt the fragrance of your
perfume, and I can't get a hold of myself. . . .*
                                    ~Trey Songz

"Valencia, you can't just lie in the bed all day,
honey. Besides working at the shop, what else
are you doing besides crying yourself to sleep
and eating everything in the house? I'm on my
way over there."

Terrell had been calling my phone all weekend, and I finally answered. I was trying to just
deal with this mess with Sean the best way that I
could, and I lasted only about two weeks before
the breakdown snuck up on me. I was at home,
trying to sort my life out, and it hit me out of nowhere that on some real shit I could be signing
divorce papers soon. Sean had been beating my
phone down for days, and even though he said
he wanted to make it work, I wasn't ready to deal

with him just yet. I stood him up for our marriage counseling appointment, because I wasn't ready to admit that we needed outside help just yet.

Sitting at the island in my kitchen, I looked at the mess I'd created in here. I counted five . . . no, six, empty containers of Häagen-Dazs butter pecan on the counter, next to several jars of dessert topping and a half-eaten Mississippi pecan cake that I'd scooped up from ShopRite on my way home from the salon Saturday night. The remnants of a twenty-four-count snack pack of chips rested on a table, and the empty bags were scattered across the floor, like a wind had come through and blown them over. I hadn't showered at all since then, and here I was on Monday afternoon, looking and probably smelling a mess.

Terrell didn't even give me the option of telling him to stay home, and although I knew he was on his way, I didn't even budge to try and clean the shit up. I wasn't in the mood. This was what I'd been reduced to—a smelly, nappy-headed, heartbroken, fat girl who was ready to go to the hotel and hunt Sean's car down. I imagined what I would do if I saw his car. I pictured myself having a *Waiting to Exhale* moment as I climbed onto the roof of his ride and started with the back window first.

A smile spread across my face as I envisioned the glass flying everywhere and hotel security coming down as the alarm screeched. I would dress in all black and would cover my face with a bandanna so that they couldn't identify me. I would hop down from his car and jet to mine, where I would ditch my outfit in the trunk and drive out of the hotel like nothing had ever happened, passing his car on the way out.

A knock at my back door brought me out of my musing, and the smile that was on my face instantly turned into a frown. I swear I did not feel like dealing with this mess today, but I had no choice but to let Terrell in, because I knew he wouldn't leave. Still, I didn't budge from the chair as he knocked again on the glass, harder this time to ensure that I indeed heard it. I just didn't want to be bothered, and I didn't feel like talking about Sean.

"Diva, I know you heard me knocking on this door," came Terrell's voice from behind me. I totally forgot I had given him a spare key to the house. I never told Sean that, because I knew he would flip.

"I was coming. You didn't give me enough time," I responded, suddenly conscious of my appearance. I could see the look of sorrow and pity in my friend's eyes, and it made me feel even worse.

"Valencia, what's really going on with you, and why are you looking like that? What is going on in this kitchen?" Terrell inquired as he began to gather the empty chip bags from the floor and table and to clear the counter of its clutter. I almost lost it when he threw the rest of my cake away, but he did the right thing. Had it sat there, I definitely would have finished it off before the night was out.

"Sean cheated on me with his assistant because I'm fat."

Speaking those words was so painful that it instantly brought tears to my eyes. The reality of the situation was that I had put on weight, but that was only part of the problem. I'd always said that the things you did to get me were the things you had to do to keep me. Sean hadn't changed; I was the one who had flipped the rules around. It had started with a gained pound here and there, and being too tired to, at the very least, give up a blow job. Long hours at the shop had strained our relationship even further, and with him being out of town all the time, I should have been more available. Hell, I'd practically handed him over to her.

She was the one I gave all my secrets to. I told her what he liked for his birthday and what to buy, until it got to the point where she had ev-

erything memorized and I didn't need to tell her
how to please my man anymore. On our anniver-
sary she made reservations for us to have dinner
at his favorite restaurant and then took my place
when I was stuck at the shop and didn't show
up. Many late nights she made sure dinner was
prepared for him when he got home, along with
having his itinerary already printed and ready to
go in his Louis Vuitton briefcase. She made sure
that his clothes were picked out for work the next
morning and that his bags were packed for business trips, and when I finally did show up, I was
too tired to at least suck his dick. I gave her my
life and made it easy for her to climb into my bed
over and over again.

His only request was for me to lose weight. It
was bad enough that I hardly had time for him,
but when I did show up, I wasn't half the person
I used to be. In fact, I'd doubled in size and attitude, and who wanted to deal with that? We
used to cuddle and share our dreams, and now
we could both barely stand the sight of each
other. This shit hurt like hell, and I wanted to fix
it. Where did I start, and how did I start over?
Was it too late?

"Have you thought about going to see a psychiatrist?" Terrell asked as he washed the last
dish in my sink and began to sweep the floor.

I knew how much Terrell hated a mess, because he kept an immaculate household. It embarrassed me that he even had to see my home like this. I always kept my house in order, but lately I hadn't really cared about that, or much else.

"A psychiatrist? I'm not crazy, Terrell. I'm overweight and depressed. That's not the same thing," I said with way more attitude than I intended. I didn't need a psychiatrist. I needed a personal trainer.

"You don't have to be crazy to lie on the couch. It's just a way of getting some things off your chest, and talking to someone that doesn't already know you and can't judge you."

"But I'm not crazy. . . ."

"I never said you were. I'm just saying that an unbiased opinion never hurt anyone. Maybe you should just give it a shot at least once. Hell, it couldn't hurt, and if you don't like it, you can always not go back," Terrell explained as he pulled a straightening comb from his bag. "Besides, once you figure out what's going on with you, you can figure out how to fix your marriage."

"But I'm not—"

"Crazy. I know. You do, however, look a mess, though. Please go shower and wash your hair so that I can get into that kitchen. Your neck is looking a tight mess, but Mother is here to make it all better. Now, hurry, because I don't have all day."

I reluctantly moved myself from the stool I was perched on and dragged my tired body up the stairs and to the bathroom. Standing in front of the full-length mirror, I took my clothes off and examined the new body that I was dragging around. Although my breasts were still only a handful, they were now sagging and were no longer their former perky selves. I grabbed at the globs of flesh that formed a spare tire around my midsection, and counted the love handles down my sides. Turning around to view the back of me, I saw that my ass was even bigger than it was before, but it wasn't a round, tight bubble anymore. Now it looked dented and flabby, and the cellulite that covered my thighs was a mess.

Standing under the stream of water that came from multiple showerheads, I cried, allowing my tears to mix in with the water and suds that ran down my body and disappeared into the drain. If I could fit down that drain behind them, I wouldn't think twice about getting washed away. After washing my body several times, I applied generous amounts of shampoo to my hair and began to scrub away my troubles. I had to take charge of my life again, and by the time I got through combing conditioner through my silky tresses and rinsing my body for the last time,

I felt like I was at least ready to take the next step—whatever that was.

Moving a little faster, so as not to keep Terrell waiting any longer, I dried and moisturized my body, saying good-bye to the extra pounds along the way. After stepping into a wife beater and a pair of sweats, I rubbed the towel through my hair as I went back down to the kitchen, where Terrell had made me a healthy lunch and had set up a station to get my hair done.

"Now, diva," Terrell began as he took an extra hot blow-dryer through my hair, "my friend Alex is real down to earth and very open and objective. He's been a therapist forever and will help you get through these trying times. I spoke to him on your behalf already, and he will be expecting you in his office tomorrow at two."

"Damn, how you just going to set up an appointment without asking me?" I asked with an attitude, yelling over the sound of the dryer.

"Because you wouldn't make the decision yourself. I have an outfit in that bag over there for you to wear as well."

For the first time since Terrell had come in, I noticed a garment bag hanging over the side of one of the kitchen chairs. I had to get dressed up to go to therapy? What was wrong with my sweatpants and a T-shirt? I hadn't been shopping in a while, and all the clothes I owned I couldn't fit into anymore, but that was beside the point.

"Why do I have to get jazzy to go to therapy?" I asked as I shrank back from the hot comb nearing my neck. I feared getting burned and didn't buy into the tale that it was just the heat I was feeling.

"You're not getting jazzy. You're turning into the new you," Terrell replied as he worked his magic on my hair. "You'll be giving up those sweatpants and T-shirts for everyday clothes. You will be looking like you own a shop from here on out. You will show Sean what he has been missing as you get back to where you want to be or close to it."

"Okay, but . . ."

"No buts. We're going to do this thing together, and I'll be right by your side. Now, hold your ear down so I can get up around that side. Don't you ever let your hair get like this again."

Terrell took his time flat ironing my hair until it was bone straight, then pinned it up into a beehive for me so that I could wrap it in a scarf until tomorrow. He offered to go with me to my appointment, but I declined. It was time for me to stand up and start taking steps on my own. I was ready to begin a new life, and I knew I had to start this journey alone. I did promise him that we could go shopping for more clothes after my session and that I would meet him at the shop.

He took the liberty of clearing my book and rescheduling my regulars for the next day. Those that couldn't wait, he would take care of for me, and we were to meet at the mall.

I was so nervous when I woke up the next day, but instead of drowning my nervousness in junk food, I took the opportunity to clear my kitchen of all of my comfort food. When I was done, I hopped on the treadmill for an hour, vowing to stick with a regular exercise routine on a daily basis until I at least got down to a size fourteen. I liked my body at that size, so that would be my aspiration.

By one o'clock I was ready to go, but I was a little depressed at the tag size of the dress I was wearing. The dress was fierce, no doubt, but I didn't like that number eighteen, which was more confirmation of my weight gain. I was on point, though, and with a touch of gloss to my lightly made-up face and the perfect high heels to match my bag, I was ready to make moves. Taking one last look in the mirror, I cleared my mind of all negative thoughts and tried to keep an open mind about this therapy thing. I wasn't crazy, and I didn't need it, but I knew I had to take steps if I wanted to move forward. It was now or never.

Emotional Roller Coaster

Yesterday I told myself I was gonna be okay. Gonna start a new day, be truly happy. I was gonna take control of me. . . .
                                            ~Vivian Green

Dr. Alexander Thornton III

Wow. That was the very first word that popped into my head when I saw her. Curvaceous, cinnamon colored, thick in all the right places. She had the prettiest face I'd seen in a while, and she was here to see me because her confidence was in question. They all saw me for the same reason. Either they gained weight and were now miserable because of it, or they lost weight and still couldn't find themselves. At the end of the day it was all the same.

I'd always loved a woman with meat on her bones. It was just sad because not too many of them seemed to know the power that they held.

I loved to see the confidence in their walk when their swagger was at its peak. It told the world that they knew who they were and what they were capable of. You had to look closely, though, because some had their head held high, but if you looked into their eyes, you could see the uncertainty. This one was a little more confident than the others. She wasn't pulling on her clothes or constantly fussing with her hair. She didn't seem fidgety just yet, so maybe a breakthrough was in the near future.

I pretended like I was hard at work reading files when my assistant buzzed me to let me know my two o'clock appointment had arrived. I could see her through the open door of my office. I preferred that view when my clients walked in. I liked to see them when they first arrived because you could tell a lot about someone by their appearance. Most of the time—let's say, 98 percent of the time—I was dead-on with my first thoughts about a person. The other 2 percent surprised me, but that rarely happened. I could tell instantly, most times, if I could help a person out or if I should call it quits immediately. I didn't believe in dragging out sessions for the sake of getting paid, and I showed my clients that rather than telling them. That way neither of us wasted time.

My assistant's voice came over the intercom. "Dr. Thornton, your two o'clock has arrived. Are you ready for her?" Was I ready for her? She was gorgeous, but I was still nursing an old wound from my last try at love. Besides that, I always kept everything strictly professional.

"Yes, send her in," I responded as I opened her file. My good friend Terrell had sent her to me and had given me a little info about her, which I had in my notes. That was his opinion, though, and didn't really count. What I needed to know I would get directly from her.

I could see her every move from the time she got up, and she was killing the dress she had on. Terrell's description of her did her no justice. My eyes traveled her curves discreetly, all the way down to her shoes, which matched perfectly the bag she held in her hand. I didn't see a ring on her finger, and I had noted that she was indeed married. I made another note to ask her about that. I could smell her perfume before she got to me, and it filled the space of my office pleasantly. It smelled like she was wearing Calvin Klein's CK One Summer 2010, but I could be wrong. Whatever it was, it went nice with her chemistry.

"Valencia McCoy-King, it's nice to meet you." I stood and greeted her with a handshake and had to keep from closing my eyes and enjoying her touch. She had baby soft hands, and at this level of closeness, she looked delicious.

"Nice to meet you as well," she replied in a voice that was music to my ears.

Who would hurt something so fragile and precious? If she was mine . . . Lord, I had to put my professional hat back on before I forgot what I was here for.

"I'm glad you were able to make it today. Is this your first time seeking out any type of therapy?" I asked her, jotting down notes in the meantime. I had a pretty basic list of questions I went through before getting to the root of the problem, and this hopefully put the person at ease about being here in the first place.

"Yes, it is. It was suggested by a friend as a good move to make, so here I am."

We both knew that Terrell was the friend she was referring to, so there was no need to go into that. I had to clear my head so that I could help her out. A part of me didn't want to hear her story, because I had heard it so many times from so many different women. Or maybe she would be a part of the 2 percent that surprised me. Hopefully, I'd be able to help her with whatever it was.

"I agree, and whatever it is you need to get off your chest, feel free. This is a judgment-free zone, and the sessions are usually an hour," I said to her, breaking down how the sessions worked and the cost of each. I also informed her that it was up to her how many sessions she attended, and how often. I didn't make that decision for people unless it was absolutely necessary.

"So, let's start with the basics," I said to her to help loosen her up. "What's the one thing that's bothering you the most?"

"Well," she began hesitantly. "I'm thinking about divorcing my husband."

"And the reason behind those thoughts is?"

"I caught him cheating on me with his assistant," she said with a straight face. My heart went out to her. I was in the very same situation not too long ago, so I knew that kind of hurt all too well. Why couldn't people just stay faithful?

"And how did that make you feel?" I asked her, already knowing the answer. She probably wanted to kill his ass.

"It made me feel like I could have done something different to prevent it. He said that I had gained too much weight and he wasn't attracted to me anymore."

I was blown. She wasn't nearly as big as I'd seen a person get, but I didn't know where she had come from as far as sizing went. Looking at her now, I decided the weight didn't look bad on her at all. I personally liked them a little fluffy. She was obviously deeply scarred from this, and I knew I had to help build her back up before some user came along and hurt her even more.

"What was your weight before? Or if that's uncomfortable, what size did you wear, as opposed to the size you wear now?"

"When I met Sean, I was a solid size twelve, to say the least. Now I'm in this eighteen, and I don't like it."

I jotted down a few questions on my pad that I would ask her down the line, and I started to chart a plan to help her get back to being happy. I just had to tread lightly and make sure happy was where she wanted to be. Some people were content with being at the bottom. I would need at least one more session to determine if that was the case with her or not, and right now I couldn't determine what it was that she wanted to accomplish.

The first meeting was always hard because the person seeking the therapy had to build up trust with a complete stranger in order to let him or herself go. Sometimes that could take a few visits; sometimes by the end of the first visit, he or she was ready to open up more. Valencia was the type that needed a to-do list, so once I gathered more info, I would know what I needed to do to get her moving in the right direction. I just couldn't get over how pretty she was, and I had to see the guy that would cause her so much pain.

"Valencia, can I speak frankly with you?" I asked. Therapist/psychiatrist aside, I liked for people to see the human side of me. Everyone got hurt sometime, and I was not immune to that. In order for her to want to open up, she needed to see the real me.

"Sure. That's what I expect from you."

"Cool. In order for me to help you, I need you to be straight up and to keep it real with me. I'm here to help you, and there is nothing you can say that I haven't already heard," I said with a smile. "You can be yourself here. Cry and scream if you need to. At the end of it all, I'm here to help you. Take as long as you need to build up your trust. Just rest assured that whatever you say here stays here. I know Terrell recommended you, and you can rest assured that I will not discuss anything we say with him."

Valencia looked like she was on the verge of breaking down, and pretty soon the tears started to fall. The human side of me wanted to get up and take her into my arms, kissing her tears away until she felt better. My professional side simply offered her a tissue and waited until she got herself together before we continued. I swear, if I had the chance, I would never purposely hurt her.

"Are you okay?" I asked sincerely before I resumed questioning her.

"Yes, I'm okay. I've been trying to hold it together since yesterday."

"No need to apologize," I said and then jumped right into my questions. "Now, tell me how you started to gain weight."

"Well," she began after blotting the corners of her eyes dry and quickly moistening her lips with her tongue.

I would have given anything to be her lips right then.

"I own a hair salon, and it's pretty packed on a daily basis, so I put in long hours. That leads to my not getting home until the wee hours of the morning sometimes, and by the time I get to sleep, it's time to get back up. This leaves me no time to go to the gym, and my food choices are even worse."

"I can imagine. Most stylists kind of eat in a rush, and everything is fast food," I responded as I jotted down more notes on the to-do list I was creating for her. Valencia needed to learn how to balance everything out, and I had an idea that might just help her in that area.

"Also, I wear sweats and tees on a daily basis, so when you have nothing to button up, you kind of go for broke." She laughed a sad laugh that pulled at my heartstrings. "My husband mentioned my weight once or twice, but I didn't really pay it any attention until recently."

"And are you happy with the way you look right now?" I asked her with a straight face. I thought she was stunning, but that was just my opinion. She looked away and tucked her lip into her mouth, like she was trying to control her tears. Then she put her head down, breathing heavily before wiping the corner of her eye again.

"Can't say that I am," she responded, biting her bottom lip.

I assumed that was to hold back more tears. I hated to see any woman in tears, but there was something special about Valencia that really made my heart go out to her. Almost like I wanted to save her from herself.

"What I'm going to do . . ." I began as I jotted down a few more notes on her chart, afterward reaching for a pen and a notepad for her to write on. I made my clients write their own notes, making them responsible for whatever it was they had to get done and to give them the chance to ask questions about anything that wasn't exactly clear.

"What do you mean, what you're going to do?" she asked nervously as she took the pen and pad I handed her.

"No need to worry. We're just going to make a small to-do list to get you started on being a happier you," I replied as I broke down the list I had for her into a few sections so as not to overwhelm her with too many things to do at once. She looked like she wasn't sure about what was going to happen, but I knew once I got her going, she would be more comfortable. "So, the first thing we are going to work on is time management. How many hours a day do you work at the shop?"

"It depends on the time of month and the day of the week. Naturally, it's busier around the holidays."

"Okay, so besides the holiday times, I want you to give me a realistic time when you can stop working and get home with enough time to get yourself together. Since you are the salon owner, I know you have certain duties, but I know you also have a manager to hold things down when you're gone. Now is the time when you are going to rely on them to actually do their job."

"Ummm . . . yes, Terrell is my manager."

"Perfect. So let's start off with you setting up all your appointments so that you can be done at the shop at six in the evening, at the very latest, with the exception of your busiest days, which are more than likely Friday and Saturday. That way you have a goal in mind, and you can fit in your workout in the evening."

"Wow, I guess you aren't playing," she said with a slight frown on her face. "When do you want me to start doing this?"

"Tomorrow. When you walk into the shop, I want you to adjust your book to fit those hours. That way once it's implemented, you can make it happen on a daily basis. Maybe consider spreading out some of your newer clients among the others in the shop or hiring a new stylist. You're the owner, so you're making the money either way."

"Wow, okay," she responded as she took notes on her pad. I was going to add to the list, but I figured that would be enough for now.

"Also, do you have a gym membership?"

"No, but I do have an in-house gym."

"Get a gym membership. That way you are surrounded by people with the same goal in mind, and you can stay motivated. I want you to try and get there, at the very least, three times a week, and I want you to do whatever type of workout you decide on for an hour. This is going to help you keep and follow a schedule."

"Okay. What else?" she replied, suddenly eager to get started.

I liked this kind of drive in people. "That's it for now. If you feel like you want to come back for another session, you can make an appointment with my secretary before you go. I have a list of things for you to do, but I want to slow walk you so that everything fits in order and doesn't knock you off your square."

"Okay. That's fine," she said.

Her smile blew my mind. I was glad that I was able to produce such a beautiful thing. "I'm always available, and no question is too crazy or minimal. How do you feel about the session so far?"

"I feel like I'm ready to get my life back."

"Good, and I'm ready to help you get there. I'll see you next week."

"Yes, you will," she replied.

She gathered her belongings and sauntered out of my office. I had to sit back and gather myself before I got up. Valencia was a definite turn-on, and I knew I had to be delicate with her. After jotting down more notes, I closed up her file and smiled, anticipating the next time I would see her.

Ms. Stress

It's better that it hurts. It's better that it feels this way to me. I can't get too comfortable, 'cause loving you is not my destiny. . . .

~Floetry

I was in the zone when I left the therapist's office. I felt liberated, almost like I could conquer anything. I still wasn't quite sure what I was going to do about the situation with Sean and me, but I did know what I wasn't going to put up with. We now had a trust issue. I felt like if he'd cheat on me with his assistant, then anyone else was game. I had to come to a decision quickly about whether I wanted to call it quits or not, and a part of me was leaning heavily toward wrapping things up so that I could get on with my life.

I didn't want to go through the motions for the duration of whatever it was that we had left. Before I kicked him out of the house, every time he left the house or didn't answer a call or his flight didn't land on time, I would be thinking he was with another woman or back with his assistant. I loved Sean, but I didn't have the energy to live like that. I also didn't feel like wasting time in couple's therapy, listening to a whole bunch of empty promises that he would be able to keep only for a few weeks, at the most. He wasn't attracted to me. That was it in a nutshell, and even if I could get the weight down, it would take me a while. It wouldn't happen overnight, especially since I didn't gain the weight overnight. I wasn't sure if Sean was built to go through the struggle with me.

I sat in my car for a while before pulling off, looking at the to-do list that the psychiatrist had given me to start on. I was so used to running on empty and staying at the shop until the wee hours of the morning. Business was booming, and just maybe I needed to pass some of the work on to the other stylists, like the psychiatrist said, and do something for me. I was always neglecting myself, which was part of the reason why I was as big as a house now. Jotting down a few notes on the notepad he gave me, I began to get excited again about my life. I needed to revamp some aspects of my life starting today.

Dialing Terrell up, I informed him that I was out of the session and would meet him at the mall as planned. I was ready for a new look, and although I'd gone from New York & Company to Ashley Stewart, I knew I could still rock it with the best of them. As I zoomed along the highway to King of Prussia, it felt good that I was not heading that way to go to the shop and work. I was actually going to do something for me, and I would make sure not to go anywhere near that end of the mall. I would deal with work tomorrow. Today I would be making good use of my black card.

I was able to find parking in a matter of minutes and decided to get started on shopping and not to wait until Terrell was able to get away from the shop. He sent me a text letting me know that he was finishing up with one of my clients and that he would be over within the hour. That gave me time to look in a few shoe stores, where I found a few pairs of fierce sandals that I was ready to wear immediately. It had been ages since I'd purchased anything for myself besides a bigger pair of sweatpants, and it felt great. I came out of Steve Madden just in time to see Terrell looking around for me. Pulling my phone from my purse, I saw that he had called a few times, but my phone was still muted from the therapy session.

"Diva, what took you so long?" I asked as I walked up behind him, loaded down with bags. I knew I would have to take a trip to the car, because I had too many bags and I had yet to go clothes shopping. Besides, I would need to change my shoes, because the heels I had on would not get me far in this mall for too much longer.

"Had to find parking, but I see you wasted no time burning a hole in that black card." He smiled at me, giving me a hug. He seemed kind of sad, though, and I decided that once we got back from the car, we would find a seat in the food court and talk.

"Well, walk me to my car so I can come up out of these shoes and put this stuff in my trunk."

Yeah, there was definitely something wrong with Terrell. He loved nothing more than walking around the mall with a million bags so that everyone would know he was balling, but today he didn't even put up a fight. I was on a high right now and didn't want to crash the mood, but I would get down to it before the end of the day. Once we got to the car, I popped the trunk, and before placing my bags inside it, I traded my heels for cute flats that would be more comfy to walk in yet still matched my outfit. I almost forgot how much I loved fashion, and I was ready to tear the mall up looking for the latest. Still, I couldn't get the look Terrell had on his face off my mind, and I just had to ask what was up.

"What's on your mind?" I asked him nervously. I wasn't in the mood for any bad news, but if I had to hear it, I wanted to get it before I started shopping. That way, if it was something disturbing, I could shop my frown away.

Instead of responding, he pulled out a folded piece of newspaper and handed it to me. I knew this was going to be bad, and about Sean, if it was in the news. Lord, what was that man up to? I started to just put the article in my pocketbook for later, but something told me to take a look at it. Nothing could prepare me for what I was about to read, and as soon as I scanned the first line, my mouth fell open. Apparently, Sean had broken up with me and had moved on to someone else. To say I was shocked was an understatement. Just last week he was talking to me about counseling, and today he was plastered all over the damn newspaper with some skinny chick.

"It's on the Internet, too, girl," Terrell said, reading my mind.

I felt like I wanted to crawl up into a hole and die. How could he do this shit to me? Wasn't my catching him in the act enough? Pulling out my phone, I dialed his number, and instead of it ringing, I was greeted by a recording telling me the number had been changed to one that was unlisted. That just made my blood boil even more.

"Diva, I know you're hurting—" Terrell began, but I held up my hand to stop him mid-sentence. I just needed to get home to see what was going on. He didn't say another word; instead, he took my car keys from my hand and got in the driver's seat, pointing my car toward my home.

I held my tears in check the entire ride, but it felt like I was five seconds from an explosion, and I had to keep myself from going down to the hotel to find Sean. It felt like it took us forever, and when we finally did pull up in front of the house, my world continued to spiral out of control. In the back, by the door, sat several bags of luggage, and I knew what was in them without having to look inside. Sean had packed up my shit and put me out. I was confused because the alarm company hadn't called and told me there was a breach, but Sean was powerful and undoubtedly had found a way to get around that.

Pulling out my phone, I called down to the Sheraton to speak to Sean, but the receptionist informed me that he had checked out early that morning. It was at times like this when I wished I had superpowers. I swear I would fly to wherever he was and beat the hell out of him. I felt myself beginning to hyperventilate, but I pulled it together. This would not be the end of this.

"Terrell, do me a favor and call your cousin up. Tell him I need him to bring his moving truck here ASAP. I have some cleaning I need to do."

Instead of being upset, I called the alarm company to reset the password, pretending like I forgot it. After they disarmed the system, I broke the glass in the back window—after realizing that my key no longer worked—and made my way into the house. Within an hour, Terrell's cousin showed up with a huge truck, and I began to remove everything from the house that I wanted to take with me, finding out in the process that Sean hadn't even have the courtesy to pack all of my stuff up.

It took a little over two hours and every piece of luggage in the house, but I held my tears in check. Once everything was out that I wanted, I allowed the moving men to help themselves to anything they wanted in the house. They cleaned up, and I urged them to take whatever was left, even if they ended up selling it. At this point I didn't care, and it showed. I gave the moving men directions to my old house, glad that I'd been smart enough not to sell it. When Sean and

I moved in together, I was going to get rid of it, but Sean insisted on making it a rental property instead of selling it to keep a cash flow coming in. It was just something I never got around to, and I simply paid the taxes on it every year. Now I was very thankful I still had it around.

Taking one last look around the house, I ended up in the kitchen. I was definitely hurt and confused, but I didn't want to deal with it at the moment. Instead, I removed the house keys from my key ring and my wedding rings and laid them on the kitchen counter. He would see them if and when he came back.

Resisting the urge to destroy the place, I set the alarm with a new code, giving the alarm company the number to Sean's office, to contact in case of an emergency. One of Terrell's cousins went out and purchased a piece of window glass to replace the piece I knocked out, and it was fixed by the time we were done. I wanted to cry, but I had to hold it together. Locking the door behind me, I knew that this would be my last time stepping foot into this place. I also knew that I would be bright and early for my next therapy session.

As I sat in the passenger seat of my car while Terrell drove me across town, I felt like I was having an out-of-body experience. What had

I done in the past that was so jacked up that when it came back around, I had to go through this? I felt like I could pull my hair out from the roots, but I kept my composure. I didn't have the energy at the very moment to spaz the way I wanted to, and I just needed to get in the house and in the bed.

It took the moving men about an hour to get all of my stuff unpacked and in the house, and I made sure to tip them very nicely for coming on such short notice. Terrell wanted to stay, but I assured him that I was cool. I just needed to be alone for a second. He finally left, and once I had the house locked up, I was able to sit down and think.

I had to have been at the dining room table forever, because by the time I finished my bottle of wine, it was dark outside. Staggering a little, I grabbed my phone and made my way toward the stairs. Halfway up, my phone rang, but the number wasn't one that I recognized.

"Hello?" I answered, trying not to slur my words. I was faded, and I felt a little dizzy, taking a seat on the bench in the hall before I fell over.

"Are you ready for that counseling session now?" came Sean's voice over the phone.

I held the phone out and looked at it like it was a foreign object before placing it back to my ear.

"Sean, go fuck yourself," I said more calmly into the phone than I appeared, before snapping the phone shut, then turning it off completely, because he kept calling back. Calling Terrell from my emergency cell phone, which I kept for moments like this, I told him that my other phone would be off for a few days, and if he wanted to reach me, the emergency phone was the one I would pick up.

Lying down in the bed, I continued to wonder how my life had got to be such a mess. As I drifted off to sleep, I could feel tears burning my eyes and sliding down the sides of my face, but I refused to give in to grief, and I allowed sleep to overtake me. I would deal with this another day. I didn't feel like putting my life back together at this moment, and I was too drunk to have any rational thoughts, anyway.

Shoo Fly

*But you need to know, you gon' have to
let go. You won't ever be me, and he won't
ever be yours. . . .*

                                                        ~Syleena Johnson

I stayed out of the shop for the rest of the
week. Not that I was an emotional wreck or anything like that. I just didn't feel like being bothered. The fact that I wasn't all balled up in a corner, sniffling and tearing, had me concerned the
most. Was I so far removed from my marriage
that I didn't care anymore? Who was I kidding?
I felt like I was near death. I just didn't have any
more tears to waste on it.

I occupied my time by unpacking my boxes
and dusting. That worked for a few hours, and I
was actually able to get a lot done. That was until
I pulled out a box of photos of me and Sean. At
first I sat the box to the side, determined to get
my mind off of him, but somewhere along the

line I ended up with a fresh bottle of wine and pictures of us scattered across the table in front of me.

Picking up the pictures one at a time, I studied each one closely, wondering when things had started to go haywire. In the beginning pictures, I could see the excitement in both our eyes and the sincere happiness behind our smiles. I could recall each moment that was captured in each picture, down to the exact time of day. I smiled to myself, remembering that I had been meaning to put the snapshots of our life in a photo album, which I never got around to buying.

I also noticed that our smiles became less genuine as the pictures got more recent. Full-body pictures showing all my curves became shots above the breasts, and Sean's smile was completely replaced with a seriously unhappy look on his face. I went from sitting on his lap in most of the pictures to sitting beside him, my waistline a little thicker. I could see unhappiness in both our eyes. Why didn't I notice it before?

I could feel the tears welling up in my eyes, and I tried to blink them back, but once I flipped open the first page of our wedding album, it was a wrap. I was so beautiful in my gown, and Sean looked equally as handsome in his tux. As I flipped the pages, happy memories from that day flooded my mind, and I could almost hear the music—reminiscent of our first date in Puerto Rico—that played from the live Spanish band that Sean had hired. I felt good looking at the pictures, up until I got to a photo of us with Sean's assistant. That put a definite damper on my mood immediately.

Taking the picture from the page, I held it up so that I could really see. Had she always been the conniving bitch I found screwing my husband on my bed? All our smiles matched perfectly, but I tried to read the look in her eyes. Was she being fake? At the time Sean had hired her just a few months before, and he wasn't really beat on inviting her to the wedding. I was the one that insisted that she come. After all, they would be working closely together from then on out, and she had been a great help with getting some of the wedding stuff together.

Slamming the picture back down, I leaned back in the chair while the tears just flowed. Truth was, I missed my husband and I wanted to talk to him. Getting up from the chair, I went in search of my cell phone. I hadn't turned it on since the other day, when I got home, and I hoped it had some power left, because I wouldn't be able to locate a charger at the moment. Stepping around the few boxes I had left to unpack, I spotted my phone on the love seat near the door.

I was nervous for some reason. What if he didn't want to talk to me? What if the photos I'd seen in the paper and on the Internet were old? What if he really wasn't the one that packed my bags and it was his assistant, trying to break us up? My phone couldn't power up fast enough, and I couldn't wait to reach Sean. I had it in my head that he had changed his number just to piss me off. In my heart Sean really wanted us to work, and he would stay through the weight loss. We were married in sickness and in health, and this was just one of those times when we had to fight harder to hold on to each other.

Once my phone became fully functional, it began to beep, indicating that I had voice messages waiting. I quickly connected to my in-box and was informed that I had six messages. I would begin to listen for Sean's voice, and if it wasn't him, I would skip past the message. I was losing hope, until I got to the fifth message and heard him. My heart felt like it was going to burst out of my chest as he began to talk.

"Valencia, I thought I had made a mistake," he began, sounding like he was trying to hold it together, just like I was. "I thought that we could try to make this work. The truth is, I got tired of hiding my relationship with my assistant from you. When you started to gain weight, that made it much easier to make a decision. . . ."

My heart stopped in my chest, if only for a second. Was he telling me that he and his assistant had been together before, or even ever since we got married? Did I walk into this marriage under false pretenses? I knew we didn't know each other that well when we married, but at the very least, I thought for sure that I knew he was single.

"So, with all of that said," the message continued, "I'll send you over the deed to the house. You can do with it what you want. Sell it or whatever. I won't be coming back to it. I'll also make sure you are taken care of if we can keep this breakup between us as quiet and painless as possible. . . ."

Quiet and painless? Did this man really want me to be quiet about a divorce after he had already broken up with me in front of the world? Anytime TMZ was reporting our breakup and showing him out with different women, it didn't get more painful than that. His message was still going on, but I had checked out moments before. Snapping my phone shut, I fell back into the chair I was sitting in and tried to gather my thoughts.

The time on my phone read 10:30 P.M. Who could I call at this time of night that was willing to listen and not pass judgment? I knew I could call Terrell, but he wouldn't be able to offer me the advice I needed. He would just do whatever was required to make me feel better. Getting up from the chair, I went up to my bedroom to get myself together. Upon entering it, I spotted the notepad I got from the therapist's office. His card was sitting on the nightstand.

Sitting on the side of the bed, I grabbed the card from its spot and flipped it over in my hand. The number to his cell phone was on the back. He did say that if I wanted to, I could call him at any time. Did he mean at times like this, when I felt like I was spiraling out of control? Or did he mean anytime during office hours? Would he think I was crazy if I called him now? I spun the idea around in my head for, like, a half hour before I finally got up the nerve to make the call. It was late, and I was on pins and needles, but I decided to take the plunge and just do it. What did I have to lose?

It felt like it took forever for me to dial his number, but I finally got through all ten digits. When the phone began to ring, I froze and almost couldn't breathe. I wanted to hang up, but my fingers wouldn't close the phone. What was I doing?

"Hello?" came the doctor's deep voice from the other end, and I couldn't say a word.

Emergency

Got a lady on the line screaming I'm what
she need. I done got this call a thousand
times; I'm leaving, rushing to see. . . .

~Tank

Dr. Alexander Thornton III

I was awakened out of my sleep by my cell
phone ringing. First taking a look at the clock
to decide if I would answer it or not, I figured it
might be an emergency, so just maybe I should
see who it was. I didn't recognize the number
and started to just let it ride, assuming it might
be a wrong number. Something in me made
me push the talk button, anyway. It was almost
eleven at night, so this had better be good.

"Hello? Is anyone there?"

"I'm sorry to wake you, Dr. Thornton. It's Valencia, and you said I could call you whenever I
needed to."

My heart skipped a beat. The vision of her curvy body invaded my mind instantly, and the sound of her voice sent chills down my spine. What could be troubling her this late at night that she would have to call me? I mean, I gave my number to a select few of my clients, but no one had yet to use it since that one crazy incident . . . but that was another story for another time.

"Certainly. I'm glad you called. I mean, what's wrong?" This woman had me tongue-tied, and I wasn't sure why. I knew instantly that something major must have happened with her and her husband's situation, but I wouldn't just come right out and ask.

"My husband . . . he . . . I can't believe . . ." she cried into the phone.

It tore me apart. I didn't know why I felt such a connection with her. I felt like I wanted to save her from whatever it was that was hurting her, but I had to keep things professional. The last time I fell in love with someone, it took me too long to bounce back, and I almost lost everything. I also needed to wrap this call up before I crossed the line. I was ready to get out of my bed and jet over to wherever she was and hold her. I had to hang up.

"Valencia, stop crying, okay? Just take a minute and breathe. We'll count down from ten together," I said to her in a soothing voice that would hopefully get her to calm down.

We both began at ten, and by the time we got to three, she was just whimpering softly. "Now, tell me what happened."

"I . . . when I left therapy the other day . . ." she began in a voice choked with tears that was killing me. By the time she got through telling me what happened, she was crying heavily all over again. "And when I got to the house, he had my stuff packed up and waiting by the door."

"And how did that make you feel?" I asked the question in such a clinical way that it made me feel sick to my stomach. I really wanted to ask her where the man was so I could see him about something. Most of the women I met were always locked into a relationship, or some form of one, with an undeserving man. It never failed.

"I still don't know how I feel. How could he do this to me?"

I didn't answer. I just allowed her to get all her tears out. It wasn't my job to pass judgment, but I knew I had to start getting her to see herself in a better light. She needed to get to a place where before she even got to this point in a relationship, she would recognize the signs and protect her heart.

"Valencia, I know I'm not supposed to see you until later in the week, but why don't you stop into my office first thing in the morning? I'll call my assistant and have her move some things around to fit you in, okay? I think it will be better to talk face-to-face."

"Okay," she sighed into the phone, sounding like she was trying to get herself together. "What time should I be there?"

"Come at eight. My first appointment isn't until eight thirty, but even if I have to push back some time, I will still be able to make strides. See you then?"

"I'll see you then," she responded with another sigh, this one sounding like relief. "Thank you for answering the phone."

"Thanks for trusting me enough to call. I'll see you in the morning."

Lying back in my bed, I stared up at the ceiling. What had the world come to? Valencia's situation took me back to a time when I had another patient just like her. She was gorgeous and voluptuous, with a sassy little attitude that her husband had tried to beat out of her. I really felt like I could help her see her true self, but once her husband found out that she was seeking therapy, she stopped coming. I didn't want to lose Valencia the same way.

I couldn't sleep, so I grabbed a notepad from my nightstand and began to jot down things I wanted to talk to Valencia about. I wished for a second I was jotting down plans for a date with her, but I kept those thoughts in check. I needed to get her off of my mind and stop thinking the thoughts I was thinking if I was going to help her. I didn't succumb to sleep until about two in the morning, and even then she invaded my dreams. When I woke up the next morning, I rushed through exercise and breakfast to get to the office so that I wouldn't be late. To my surprise, when I pulled up, she was just getting out of her car.

I took in her curves as she stood straight and adjusted her clutch under her arm. She was rocking the hell out of a cute pair of jeggings and a floral-printed top that caught the wind and flowed softly around her. Once she made it around to the front of her car, I could see her feet, and the sandals she chose to go with her outfit were fierce. Her long hair was loosely curled, and her face was made up nicely. There was no indication that she'd been in a middle of a meltdown just hours before. I was glad to see that she was still taking steps to pull herself together, the way we discussed, and she hadn't shown up in sweats and a raggedy T-shirt. That showed me that she was still in the race to gain her independence.

"Good morning, Valencia. Glad you could make it," I said from behind her as I walked to catch up with her. She looked a little startled when she turned around, but once she saw me, she smiled.

"Thank you so much for agreeing to see me so early. I'm sorry for any inconvenience this may have caused in your schedule."

"It isn't an inconvenience at all. I'm glad you called. That's what I'm here for."

I took in the scent of her perfume and allowed it to roll around in my nose as she went ahead of me. I wanted to close my eyes and really save it to memory, but I didn't want her to think I was a weirdo or anything like that. I did take a second to enjoy the view, though. I was a man, after all. Stopping at the receptionist's desk before going into my office, I checked for any notes or messages that might have come in after I left on Friday. Satisfied that I had gathered everything that I needed, I walked toward my office.

"Valencia, you can come in when you are ready," I said to her from the door of my office. In the meantime I took a second to get her file out, along with the notepad that I'd made notes on the night before, so that we could really talk.

I wanted to help Valencia get to a stronger place in her life.

She looked a little timid this time as she walked into my office, and I knew in her head she was wondering if she was doing the right thing. I think I might have been happier to see her than she was being here. Once she got herself settled, I pulled out a mirror and set it on my desk. We sat there for a minute, staring at each other, and I felt like I could've looked into her eyes forever. After a while I passed her the mirror on my desk, but still no words were spoken. She gave me a strange look but said nothing.

"Valencia, tell me what you see in that mirror."

She looked in the mirror for a long time without saying anything. I wished I could be in her head to hear all the thoughts that were probably fighting for the number one spot. I allowed her as much time as she needed, and I didn't stop her when the tears began to fill her eyes and fall. She was hurting, but I needed her to see her value. I needed her to know it was okay for her to cry.

"I see . . ." she began in a cracked voice as she struggled past her tears. "I see a fool. I see someone who is gullible and keeps making mistakes. I see a fat girl replacing the woman I used to be.

I see a lonely old woman," she cried out, closing her eyes for a brief second and holding the mirror to her chest.

She almost had me for a minute, but I held it together. My biggest weakness was a woman in tears.

"I see a woman ready for change, but not sure how to get there," she concluded, setting the mirror facedown on my desk.

"Valencia, pick the mirror back up and repeat after me," I instructed, never taking my eyes from her face. She looked uncertain, but I gave her a reassuring smile to let her know she could trust me. "Repeat after me," I said to her after she looked back in the mirror. "I'm an independent woman."

"I'm an independent woman?" she asked, rather than repeating the statement.

"Yes, you are. You are a business owner, and you are making moves on your own. You don't need a man to define you. Now, repeat after me. I love myself."

She looked like she wanted to start crying again. Today was crucial because it would set the tone from here on out for how she would view herself. I knew that was one of the questions that she wanted to answer right away, but she would have to feel it on the inside and believe it.

"I love myself," she said in a low voice, which I knew in time would get bolder and bigger.

"Valencia, in order for you to be prepared to accept another husband or even the one that you have, you have to come already complete. You don't need a man to complete you. He should compliment you. You are bringing 100 percent to the table, and so should he."

"How do I start over?" she asked, and the tears began again. This time I handed her a tissue.

"To start over, you have to stop everything else. If you don't like certain things in your life, be done with them and move forward. You won't make it to the finish line if you keep looking back to see what everyone else is doing."

It looked like that thought hit home with her. I didn't want to drill anything in her head, but I wanted her to see that she could do better than what her husband did to her. The thing about renewal was knowing you deserved better and doing whatever you had to do to get it and retain it. Contrary to popular belief, life was not as simple as some folks tried to make it.

"You're right. I'm ready to move forward and do what I have to do for me," she finally said, drying the corners of her eyes. "I'm ready to live life on the edge and take the next step."

"That's great to hear. Are you ready to add another task to your to-do list, or are you content with where you are?"

"The task I have in mind is not on my to-do list, Doctor."

"It's not? Good. I like to see people take the initiative. What is it that you want to take on next?" I asked, prepared to add to my notes.

"Doctor, have dinner with me tonight."

Blown! To say the very least, I was totally caught off guard and didn't know how to answer. I was honored that she chose me, but did I really want to cross that patient/therapist line? The last time I did that, the woman ended up being a crazed lunatic that I could not help. On the flip side, if I said no, rejection could set her further back. Even more so on the flip side of that, I did want to go out with her. So the question was, did I take off my professional hat and give her what she asked for, or did I stick to the script?

"You don't have to if you feel uncomfortable. It's just that I really don't want to be alone tonight, and I figured a night out would be fun. No strings attached. Just a nice dinner and possibly another therapy session." She laughed a little, with a look on her face that said that she would be okay if I decided not to go.

"I'll go on one condition."

"What's that?"

"I'll go if you let me pick the spot. I know a nice little place that has an open mic on Monday nights. You'll like it."

Instead of responding, she wrote her cell number down on a Post-it and slid it across the desk. Without another word, she gathered her pocketbook, and with her head held high, she strutted out of my office. Stopping at the receptionist's desk, probably to make an appointment, she spent a few minutes there, and then she was off. Her perfume lingered long after she was gone, and I got myself together for my next appointment.

I wasn't sure if I was crossing the line, but I was willing to throw caution to the wind and see what happened. Besides, I was just having dinner with a client, no more, no less. For some reason, though, I was excited about it, and a little nervous at the same time. It had been a while since I had been out, and although I wasn't trying to see Valencia romantically, a night out on the town would be nice.

We might actually develop a good friendship, if nothing else.

Hold It Against Me

*If I said my heart was beating loud. If we
could escape the crowd somehow. If I said
I want your body now, would you hold it
against me?*

~Britney Spears

Did I just ask my therapist out on a date? How
thirsty did that make me look? I walked out of
there with my head held high, but when I got outside of the building and to my car, I was freaking
out. What if things went wrong? Who would I see
for my therapy? And what would I tell Terrell?
They were good friends, and I didn't want any
crazy shit with me to be a potential deal breaker
with them. I didn't know what I was thinking
when I did that. It just kind of came out. I wanted
to go back inside and tell him never mind, but I
didn't have the nerve. Maybe he would decide not
to call, and I could just walk back in there for my
next appointment like nothing happened.

What was I doing? I was only a few weeks fresh off of the mess with Sean, and apparently we were headed for divorce. It was way too soon to be trying to flick up with someone else. But it was just dinner. . . . What harm could that cause? I battled with myself all the way to the mall. I wanted to look nice for Alexander tonight, but I didn't want to look like I was purposely trying to overdo it. I so wanted to call Terrell, but I didn't want to talk to him until after the dinner. Just in case things went haywire, he would know what to do.

In no time, I was able to find a sexy little number that wasn't too revealing but looked good on my body type. Once I scored a pair of shoes to match, I made my way to the spa to be pampered for the rest of the day. I didn't want to look tired and overworked; I wanted to look refreshed and happy to be there. I would also take a nap when I got back home so that I was alert and was not yawning during dinner.

I started to feel a little excitement as the day went by. I knew that the good doctor wasn't Sean and wouldn't just whisk me away to Japan at a moment's notice, and I was prepared for a regular night on the town. Who knew? Alexander might surprise me and really end up being the distraction I was looking for. I was not looking to be married again tomorrow, but I did want to enjoy myself during the healing process.

When I got home, I had some extra time, so I started to unpack a few more boxes. Alexander didn't say what time he would be ready, but I figured it would be once his office was closed for the day, and I didn't want to seem desperate by calling and asking him. He said he would call me. Once I got done with the boxes, I would shower, so by the time he did call, all I would have to do was get dressed. When I got to the table, all the photos of Sean and me stopped me in my tracks. I couldn't help but think again, where did we go wrong? I didn't dwell in the moment; instead, I brushed all the pictures back into the box that they came out of and stuck the box on top of the china closet in the dining room. I would deal with that another day. For now, I had a date to get ready for.

I'm Doin' Me

*Doin' me this time around. Doin' me, don't
need you now. I'd rather be by myself. I
won't let your drama hold me down. . . .*
                                        ~Fantasia

I was a nervous wreck as time ticked by. It
was already almost eight o'clock, and I'd been
certain that Alexander and I would at least be
sitting down for dinner by now. I didn't want to
come off as thirsty and desperate by calling him,
but I was starting to think he'd stood me up. I
was so kicking myself now for even asking him
out, and I had a bottle of wine on tap just in case
I needed to drink away my sorrows. I tried not
to overthink the situation, but I knew his office
had closed hours ago. Maybe he went home to
change? Maybe he didn't know how to break the
date off gently?

As I paced back and forth in front of my bed,
eyeballing the fierce outfit I had just purchased

for the night, I wondered briefly what the return policy was. I tried not to look at the clock and ended up having to unplug it so that I wouldn't be watching the time tick by. I called my cell phone from my landline several times to be sure that the phone was working properly, and I was starting to lose it. I didn't want to peg Alexander as a regular man, but I swear all men were turning out to be exactly the same.

Just as I felt like my life was coming to an end, and the tears started to spill down my face, my cell phone rang. A part of me wanted to ignore it and let the shit go to voice mail, but I really wanted to hear what Alexander's excuse would be. Scrambling for the phone, I first looked at the caller ID to see who it was. If it wasn't Alexander, the call would be going to voice mail. Glancing at the number on the screen, I immediately didn't recognize it and started to ignore the phone. Then I thought maybe his cell phone had died and maybe he was calling me from a landline. Either way, I needed to decide what I was going to do before the call went to voice mail.

"Hello?" I said into the phone, hopefully not sounding like I'd been near a breakdown just five seconds ago.

"When are we going to stop with all of this nonsense and handle this situation like adults?"

I wanted to puke instantly. Here I was, in the middle of a crisis, and the last person I wanted to hear from called my damn phone. Why was this man torturing me? I wanted to go in on his ass and tell him how I felt, but before I could get a word out, my other line beeped and Alexander's name flashed across the screen. I clicked over without even acknowledging Sean's crazy ass.

"Hello?"

"Valencia, I'm so sorry for the holdup. One of my patients went into crisis mode, and I couldn't get out of the office any earlier. Please tell me it's not too late to go to dinner. I'm ready to go. I just really had to handle things before I met up with you."

Wow. It was refreshing to meet a man who wasn't all about himself and who didn't treat me like I was lucky just to be in his presence. He actually sounded apologetic and nervous. A small smile spread across my face. I was glad to hear that it was a work crisis, and not all of the mess that I was thinking up about him.

"No, it's not too late. I figured something crazy must have happened, so I took that time to unpack," I said into the phone through my smile. "Where do you want me to meet you?"

Grabbing a slip of paper, I wrote down the address to the Melting Pot, where we would be meeting for dinner in the next hour. He was already en route, so I hung up with him and dressed quickly to meet him there. My phone rang several more times, and the caller ID screen showed the number that Sean had called me from, and I just ended up powering the phone down and grabbing the other phone instead. I didn't want him to be calling constantly during dinner.

To save time, I applied my makeup at the red lights while I made my way to downtown Philly. I felt a sense of relief and couldn't wait to get my evening started. When I got to the restaurant, I double-checked my face before exiting my car. I was pleasantly surprised to find Alexander waiting in the lobby for me, and not at a table, drinking, like Sean would have been. I had to get it in my head that Alexander was a different kind of man. I also had to keep in mind that Sean had dumped me and I wouldn't be dealing with him anymore. It was time for me to do me and enjoy my life.

Alexander gave me a nice long hug and a kiss on the cheek, like he'd missed me or something. I was amazed at how I fit right into his arms perfectly, and I didn't feel self-conscious about the extra weight I had put on. Grabbing a hold of my hand, he walked me through the restaurant as we followed the maître d' to our table. This date all of a sudden felt more personal than I wanted it to be, and I needed to pull back for a second and collect my thoughts. Once we were seated and situated, Alexander gave me his undivided attention, and any nervousness I had disappeared immediately.

"You look beautiful tonight," he began after we were seated and were given menus. "I'm sorry again about the delay earlier. I really had no time to squeeze a call in. I had to have a patient transferred to a facility, and once you are inside, all cellular devices are confiscated until it's time to go. I apologize for everything."

"No apology is needed. I knew you would keep your word," I replied, although I'd felt totally different not too long ago. I'd been ready to throw him to the wolves and dismiss him completely. It was a good thing he called when he did.

We settled into our meal, and I had so much fun. I'd never been to a restaurant where I had to cook my own food, but it was an enjoyable experience. We didn't feed each other like in the movies, but we did have a wonderful conversation that was filled with laughter. I learned about the good doctor and had to remember to call him Alex like everyone else. I was glad that the conversation didn't get all clinical, and I didn't feel at any point during the night that he was analyzing me.

He seemed like he had his head on straight and all his ducks lined up in a neat row. He wasn't all stuffy, like I assumed most doctors would be, and he had plenty of jokes, which kept me in stitches throughout the night. On the flip side I wondered about his flaws. Why was this man single?

Once dinner was through, he drove behind me all the way to my house, and once I parked, I sat in his car, where we talked for another two hours before I went inside. I was going to invite him in, but then I realized that I still hadn't gotten the house completely together, and there were still boxes and dust everywhere. He was a gentleman, though, and didn't even ask to come in. When we got out of the car, he walked me to my door and sent me off for the night with a quick embrace and a forehead kiss. That only confused me even more.

After securing the house and setting the alarm, I raced upstairs to get out of my clothes so that I could be ready when Alex called me to let me know he was home. I wasn't sure if this was considered a first date, but I was happy that it was different from what I'd had with my soon-to-be ex-husband. Alex didn't whisk me away to Morocco or anything like that, but I was content and happy with our night out. I wondered when we'd do it again.

Alex called, just like he promised, and we chatted only for a little while before ending the call. I had a therapy session scheduled for the beginning of next week, and I briefly wondered if it would be awkward. Although I'd had a ball with him, I still needed help and was in no shape to jump into anything. We probably shouldn't go out again, but I decided that if we did have another date, it would only be if he asked. I wouldn't initiate it the next time.

I was finally able to get into the bed at about midnight, and for the first time in a while I felt like I might have a good night's sleep. I closed my eyes and was on my way to dreamland soon after. Suddenly it sounded like someone was blaring their car horn outside of my house, but I simply chalked it up to a dream or to someone looking for a neighbor. Besides, who knew I was here? It wasn't until I heard someone calling my name that I knew I wasn't dreaming and sat up in the bed.

Getting up from the bed, I dragged my body over to the window to see what was going on. When I pulled the curtains back, I was shocked to see Sean standing outside of my house. What was he doing here? I really didn't feel like going through it with him tonight, but I knew that if I didn't talk to him, he would never leave.

"What do you want, Sean?" I asked him through the window screen. Damn, I didn't feel like this shit tonight.

"We need to talk about us. Open the door," he demanded, not waiting for a reply and walking up to the door. Sighing, I pulled the curtains closed and prepared for battle, because I knew Sean wouldn't make this easy.

What Goes Around

*First of all you should know I am over you,
it's okay. But then again I never thought
I would make it to this day. After everything we've been through I finally know
the truth. . . .*

~Lalah Hathaway

When I got downstairs to the door, I hesitated
for a brief second before opening it. Why was
this man in my face? I was trying my best to
move past him and get on with my life, and here
he came, wanting to drag things out. Hell, he'd
locked me out of my own house and changed
the pass code. That indicated to me that he had
moved on, too. What else was there to think?

Deciding to just get this conversation over
with, I opened the door and walked over to the
couch, not fully acknowledging that he was
there. No hello or anything. I really didn't have
much to say, to be totally honest, and figured

I'd just hear him out and then he could leave. I also knew things wouldn't go that smoothly. As I took him in, the scent of his cologne took me back to the days when I thought we were in love. He looked damn good, too, but then I quickly remembered that he wasn't attracted to me anymore, and pushed those thoughts out of my mind. We didn't have a snowball's chance in hell of getting back together if I had anything to do with it.

"What is it that we need to discuss, Sean?" I asked through a yawn. I was already bored with the situation and wasn't beat for the bullshit.

"Wow, is that how you greet your husband after not seeing him after all this time?" he asked with a smile on his handsome face.

I wasn't anywhere near cracking a smile. "How can I help you, Sean?" I asked, looking like I'd rather be in bed than sitting here, dealing with this mess.

"Okay, I see you want to get straight to the point," he responded, shocked at my candor. "I came to talk to you about coming back home."

"Not interested. Anything else?"

"Damn, Valencia, is it like that?"

Silence said a thousand words, so I decided to let that thought sink in. I didn't want to drag things out, and I damn sure didn't feel like a shouting match. I wasn't even over him cheating, and there he was in the damn paper and all over the Internet with random chicks. Our marriage hadn't even been dissolved, and he was already out doing his thing. I was cool on his trifling ass.

"So you're not going to say anything?" he asked.

Once again he was greeted with silence.

"You are really taking this shit to another level. What do you want from me? What do I have to do to get you back home?" he pleaded, like he wasn't dead wrong for everything.

"First of all, Sean," I said as calmly as possible. I was not about to let him think that he even remotely got up under my skin; he wasn't getting that type of satisfaction. "If I remember correctly, it was you I caught in our bed, having sex with your assistant, right? I don't remember you having a twin."

"Yeah, it was, but—"

"And it was you that I saw plastered all over the Internet and the newspaper when you announced our breakup to Media Take Out, right?"

"Yes, but I was just trying—"

"And it was you that took the liberty of packing my things and sitting them outside of our house after changing the locks and the pass code, correct?"

"Valencia, I was just trying—"

"Trying what? To piss me off? You certainly succeeded."

"All I was trying to do—"

"Was end our marriage, and it's done. All of this because I gained a few pounds?"

"To be fair, you didn't just gain a few pounds."

All of the air was sucked out of the room at that moment. Sean realized his mistake immediately, and it showed on his face. Surprisingly, I wasn't even mad. The new me didn't give a damn what he thought. I was on my way to a healthier me, and it would be too bad for him that he didn't stick around to see the end results.

"To be fair, don't ever come back here again. Have a good night."

And with that said, I got up from my seat and made my way up the stairs. I would not let him see how much what he said hurt me. At the end of the day it didn't even matter. He wouldn't have to worry about me or how many pounds I gained. It was over.

"Valencia, if I could just get a word in edgewise . . ."

"Don't let the *edge* of the door hit you in the ass on the way out."

Standing at the top of the landing, I waited for him to leave. I didn't sign up for this bullshit.

People married for better or for worse. All he did was replace me with a younger, thinner model, and I wouldn't even try to compete with that. He made his decision, and that was how we were going to move from here on out.

"Valencia, I need you in my life. I was bugging out and didn't realize what I had at home. I thought I needed to fit into a certain image, and I'm over it now. I'm willing to stay through the weight loss. I'll pay for gastric bypass, or whatever it is you want to do. Just tell me you'll think about it. You don't have to answer today."

I thought that if he came correct, I might want to make it work. But I felt absolutely nothing and just wanted him out of my house. I was standing there, looking at him, wondering what I ever saw in him. Both of us had been in our prime when we met, and we weren't prepared for times like this when things were crazy. I loved Sean, but I wasn't totally convinced anymore that I was in love with him. In my heart there was a big difference between the two.

"Valencia," Sean said as he walked closer to the steps, "please come home."

Was this fool crying? I wanted to laugh, but I didn't even have the energy for that. How many times had I sat up crying, wondering why things were the way they were between us? Sean must have bumped his head along the way or something. After what he said to me, he wanted it to work? Yeah, right!

"Sean, we don't have a home. As a matter of fact, you offered to send me the deed to our house, and you confessed that you were tired of hiding your relationship with Carla from me. That means you had been sleeping with her for a while. The very first time you stuck your dick in her ended our marriage. There's nothing I can do for you now."

"But Valencia, I just want to—"

"Sean, I want you to leave."

He looked defeated. The crazy shit was, as badly as I wanted to take joy in his misery, I just couldn't do it. I almost felt bad for him. It was like I was looking at him the same way I had when we first met, and even if I wanted to try it again, we were in different places in our lives now. I thought I would be cool with him doing his thing, because I was pretty busy myself, but apparently, I was too busy to handle my business, and I left his happiness in the hands of other women. There was no backtracking on that. I would never have another good night's sleep as long as we were together. That was the conclusion I came to.

He turned to leave, looking back at me one last time. I could see it all in his eyes. . . . He realized that he might have messed up on the best thing that had ever happened to him. That wasn't my problem now. Once the door closed, I walked back down to lock it and resisted the urge to look out the window to watch him go. By the time I got upstairs, I could hear his car start and then pull out of the driveway. Lying back down in the bed, I pulled the covers up under my chin and smiled. I was strong enough to get through this. I was ready for change, and I was ready to move on. I just had to convince my heart of the same thing.

Sometimes I Cry

I can sleep at night. I don't reach for you when I wake up, but it's taken some time. I can live my life without praying that we could make up. . . .

~Eric Benét

Eight months later

I was excited today. My appointment with my therapist was right after my workout, and I had a full book of clients ready to go. A few months ago I didn't think that I would ever get over Sean. He didn't really give me any breathing room at first. That night after he left my house, he just kept coming back. He even went as far as selling our other house and depositing the money into my bank account. Then his simple ass got mad because I withdrew the money and put the shit back in his. When I said I wanted nothing from him, I was dead serious. I wanted to be done with it all.

It took me a while, but I eventually went down to a see a lawyer who was recommended to me by my therapist. There was no use in trying to salvage the unsalvageable. I wasn't interested in doing so anymore. Besides, I finally had someone that loved this size sixteen for what it was. Yep, I said a size sixteen, and still counting down. Once I got into the rhythm of getting my life back on track and following the checklists that I made for myself on a weekly basis, I was in there. Why was I still seeking therapy? Honestly, I felt like I still wasn't ready to stand on my own and needed help staying focused. I didn't go as many times a week as I used to, but I was making progress a day at a time.

"So, Valencia, what's new on your plate to-day?" my therapist asked me. I instantly started blushing. There was so much I wanted to tell him.

"Well, I have a date tonight, so I'm excited about that. And I have a full book, so I know I'll have to work fast."

"How are you doing with managing your time?" he asked as he looked at me over his glasses and took notes.

"I'm keeping my schedule pretty tight. I have two new stylists, and I'm thinking about moving to a new location a few spaces down. Business has been really great for a while now."

"That's good to hear. I'm glad things are working out the way you need them to," he responded, smiling at me. "What about that other thing we talked about?"

I couldn't contain the smile that spread across my face. Terrell had been a real help with keeping the salon on track and running when I wasn't around. I worked only from Wednesday to Saturday, giving myself a three-day weekend to handle shop business, home business, and my personal life, and not necessarily in that order. I needed some direction, and I needed everything to be balanced. Just think, in the beginning I felt like therapy was just for crazy people, when in reality I didn't realize how off-kilter I really was.

I was able to accomplish a lot, and eventually I found the balance and the happiness that I was looking for. I heard it said once that a person should go into a relationship already complete. You should not be in search of completion, but of a complement. Your significant other was supposed to add to what you already had; that way, you were both bringing 100 percent to the table. I wasn't even aware that on a good day the very most I contributed was 65 percent, an eye-opener, for sure.

"I'm still working on it," I responded as I tried to hide my blushing face.

"That's good to hear. So far we've been able to hit consistent targets . . ." my therapist went on. I kind of daydreamed a little as he talked, and I doodled on my notepad, acting as if I was taking notes. I was ready to get up out of there, because I had a few more things I had to do, and my new friend was waiting for me in the parking lot.

"So are there any questions?" my therapist asked me.

"No, Dr. Matthews, everything is crystal clear."

"Good. I'll see you this time next week. Remember what I told you. You are—"

"Somebody!" I said, cutting him off and finishing his sentence.

Thanking him, I gathered my things up, and once I made my next appointment, I rushed out to the parking lot. Alexander got out of his car and made his way around to the passenger side to open the door for me, planting a kiss on my cheek.

I blushed again for the millionth time that day as I made myself comfortable in the passenger seat and made sure he had room to close the door. I kept my eyes on him up until he got in the car, and then I smiled widely as we moved toward our next destination.

My life was going exactly the way I had planned it, and thanks to Alexander, I saw things a lot more clearly. After that mess with Sean, Alexander and I became close, and we decided not too long ago that it would be in my best interest to seek help from another professional if we were going to date seriously. It was about morals and keeping business and personal separate. His stance on that just made me like him even more.

We chatted briefly about our plans for the night as he drove me toward the salon. My car was in the shop for repairs, and he'd volunteered to be my escort so that I wouldn't have to get a rental, and it would be an opportunity for us to spend more time together. We were taking things slow, though, and one day at a time. Looking over at him, I took in his handsome profile, from his thick lips to his neatly arched eyebrows, back to his distinctive nose. I wasn't sure how long this thing we had was going to last, but I did wonder from time to time how our children would look if we had any. It was just a fun thought to have, and it made me smile throughout the day.

"Okay, love, we're here. I'll see you around six?" he asked me as he parked the car.

"I'll be ready," I replied as I leaned in to meet him halfway. I swear this man had the softest lips on the planet, which caused all kinds of naughty thoughts to flood my mind, making me blush again.

"One day you have to tell me what you are thinking about." He smiled at me. "Every time I look at you, you're blushing and turning red."

"One day I will," I responded as I thought about the things I would do with him when I had the chance. "Have a good day."

"You do the same." He smiled as he got out of the car and circled around to let me out.

And people say chivalry is dead. Stepping into his open arms, I snuggled up close to him and enjoyed the warmth of his embrace—something that I had been missing for a long time.

After sharing another quick kiss, I stepped away from him and reluctantly went into the shop to start my day. I said reluctantly not because I didn't want to make money, but because I would have loved to just spend the day wrapped around Alexander.

"Diva!" I heard Terrell call from the back when I entered the shop.

The shop was on fire, and I was instantly in the mood to work my magic. On my way to the back I noticed a giant bouquet of tiger lilies resting on my station, and a wide smile spread across my face at the pleasant surprise.

"Hurry and open the card. I need some romance in my life," Terrell said as he rushed up to my station to be nosy.

I reached for my phone. I wanted to have it near me so that I could thank Alexander for the pleasant surprise. I had made him promise that he wouldn't spoil me, but he never listened.

Searching the bouquet, I found the card tucked neatly off to the side, the aroma of the flowers filling my nostrils in the process. I was smiling wide as I used my nails to gently lift the seal from the back so that I wouldn't ruin the envelope. I kept all the little mementos that Alexander gave me. I was feeling good at the moment, but all of that came to a screeching halt once I realized that the gorgeous flower arrangement I was admiring was not from Alexander, but from Sean. Annoyance washed over me instantly.

"Sean strikes again," Terrell commented the moment my face changed, and then he turned to address the shop. "Which one of you lucky ladies will get to take home this beautiful bouquet of flowers this week? Everyone, put your name on a Post-it note and drop it in the bag. The person's name I pull out gets to leave with it today."

Sean irritated me to the soul. It had been a while since I'd gotten a gift from him, and I still wasn't impressed. Every week he would send flowers or jewelry, and every week I would give it away to one lucky client. A month or so ago Terrell's client Dynetta lucked out and walked

out with a two-carat diamond tennis bracelet. I
didn't want a thing from him. Every card he sent
requested that I call him to talk over our relationship. I would throw each card in the trash
every time.

I was finally free from Sean, after having to
go through extra measures to have the divorce
executed because he wouldn't sign the divorce
papers. It was a mess. It didn't matter to me,
because at the end of the day I was free to do me
and be me, flaws and all.

"Ms. Bryant, you can have a seat in my chair,"
I said to my first client as I prepared my station
for the day.

Once everyone's name was in the basket, Terrell called out the winner, and we went on with
business like we always did. I loved my team,
and whether we laughed or cried, discussed
Wendy's hot topics or a topic from Oprah, or
fought with each other one minute, and then
hugged the next, we had each other. At the end
of the day I had my health, my business, and my
man. Everything a woman could ask for.

Three the
Hard Way

by

Natalie Weber

Chapter 1

Amber Couture was a woman whose five-foot-four-inch body had plenty of curves. Her long, black, straight hair was almost doll-like, and she had her mother's hazel eyes. Her complexion was light, which gave the impression that she was of Caucasian descent. But her origins were more exotic than that. Amber's mother was from Brazil. Her hair was naturally jet-black and straight, but she loved to dye it a bronze color, which made it look different shades of red and amber all meshed into one. Her hazel eyes were her first feature to be noticed, before her body. Her father was a Southern man born in North Carolina, whose parents moved to New York when he was a year old. Amber hadn't got many of her father's features, but her attitude was all him. She had his drive and ambition, along with his smarts.

Amber was the only child of Ray and Emily Couture. When she was only six, her mother died of a sudden brain aneurysm. A year later her father's parents died in a car accident caused by a drunk driver. After such devastation, Ray worked even harder to provide Amber with a loving home. She missed her mother dearly, but her father filled her life with such joy and happiness that his role of being both a mother and father to her seemed to come naturally. Her father doted on her, and she was a true daddy's girl even now, as a grown woman. Fortunately, her father owned a thriving car business in Long Island, New York, that allowed her all the luxuries a child could ever want. And, when his parents died, he relocated his business to sunny Miami, Florida.

When she became of an age to learn about her father's business, she did her very best to absorb everything he did. She'd been interested in cars from a young age, especially how they worked. Her father sent her to the best schools and even had her working as a car salesman when she was eighteen years old. From that point on there was no stopping her from becoming her father's overachiever, in more ways than one.

She arrived at her office at quarter past ten Monday morning. She adored her job. It gave her great pride to know she had control over so many men. But what she most enjoyed was when anyone tried to make a fool out of her, she quickly made them wish that they had never tested the waters. Her knowledge about luxury cars was vast. Amber could tell by the sound of the car if there was a problem with any vehicle on the lot. Her knowledge of and love for cars put her on a high with lots of benefits.

As she opened the side door to enter her office, she glanced over to the right and noticed how cute Trevor looked today. His incredibly ripped body was so profound, she would have been a fool to pass up that eye candy every day. All the salesladies came into her office just to see him. The front wall in her office was made of glass; she had a great view of the garage.

Amber sat at her desk, waiting for her computer to connect with the Internet. She peered over her computer screen, looking at Trevor's bulky biceps under his T-shirt. His skin tone was smooth as chocolate, an even tone throughout. His hair lay neatly in a circular motion around his head, forming waves like on the ocean. By looks alone, he could part any legs he wanted— including hers. She'd never understood why her father had employed Trevor. She often tried to ask her father where he came from and why he had a job at their dealership, but her father never enlightened her on that subject. All she knew was he could fix any car on the lot, and he never went to school and didn't have a college degree. Amber's daydream was quickly interrupted by the phone buzzing. Startled, she quickly picked it up, hoping no one had seen her staring. "Amber Couture speaking. How may I help you?"

"Good morning, baby girl. How you doing this morning?" Her father, Ray Couture, spoke with a distinctive Southern accent.

"Oh, am doing just fine. What's up?"

"Umm, can you make lunch today? I have someone I would like you to meet."

"What time? And it better be a good spot," Amber said with a hearty laugh.

"Wherever you like, sweetie. I need you to be on board because you are going to be his boss." Ray laughed.

"Daddy, how many jobs would you like me to handle? I just feel like you always put it on me," Amber whined.

"Because you are responsible, reliable, and you're my daughter. Just remember, this will all be yours one day, and besides, you need to know all aspects of the business, not just the parts, baby girl." Her father let out a slight chuckle at his daughter's frustration. "This is going to be easy for you. Trust me, nothing for you to be stressed out about. Just a few calls and a meeting once a week, easy as pie. Consider this as an opportunity to help give your fellow local black-owned business a push in the right direction."

"Okay, Daddy, okay. But if he fucks up once, he's out. Deal?" Amber asked, tapping her fingers on the desk.

"Now, Amber, you know how I feel about fuck-ups."

"I know, Daddy. Everyone deserves a second chance. It just shows that they need more guidance."

"Okay, we are settled, then? One o'clock good for you?" Ray asked.

"Yup, sounds good. I want some lobster salad from the country club. I will meet you there." Amber spoke with her eyes closed, licking her lips at the thought of lunch.

"Great. See you then." Her father hung up the phone.

Amber put the receiver down and wished it was already lunchtime. She looked at her watch. *Damn, only ten thirty, but I am already hungry,* Amber thought. She couldn't help that her stomach was already growling. Her appetite had plagued her most of her adult life. Amber felt like Oprah: one month she was a size eight, and the next month she was a size twelve. Now she just didn't care about it anymore; if the men didn't want her full-figured size fourteen, then to hell with them.

She snapped out of her trance about food and began her daily intake inventory online. Amber kept sneaking peeks at Trevor through her glass entrance and couldn't prevent herself from wetting her panties. She smiled at the thought of him having his way with her. She didn't care that he worked there. *I can always have him relocated if he can't handle a little fun. After all, I am his boss,* she thought.

With her thoughts on Trevor's body, she walked out to the garage. Their flirtation with each other for the past month had reached a peak, and she couldn't help but have a feel-good moment. *Shit, don't men have sidekicks all the time? Why can't I?* her mind questioned.

Trevor stepped back from the car, watching her walk by.

Amber knew Trevor had his eye on her. She walked as if she were on a runway, modeling the most elite fashion from Milan.

"Hello, Ms. Couture. How are you today?" Trevor asked, looking at her well-rounded ass.

Amber turned around. "I'm fine, Mr. Turner, and how are you?" She stared at his strong chest.

"Oh yes, you are, Ms. Couture. That you surely are." He looked around and saw his coworker on the other side of the garage, concentrating on an electronic repair for a 2011 Porsche Cayenne sport. "Ms. Couture, I would love to take you out to lunch sometime."

"Mr. Turner . . ." Amber stepped a little closer and panned the garage for anyone in earshot of their conversation. "Do you think you can afford it?" Her sexiness oozed.

"Ms. Couture, now, if I couldn't, would I ask?" Trevor said with a hint of an attitude.

"Maybe, but as you know, there is a policy at the office. No romances with coworkers. You could lose your job. Now, you know we can't have that, 'cause you would need the money to wine and dine me." Amber chuckled.

"Now, that would be a bad look, but I have other ways of wining and dining you," Trevor quickly said.

"Oh, really? And what might that be?"

"Don't you worry about that. . . . There are other ways. . . ." Trevor licked his lips slowly, hinting at his sexual desires.

"Oh, really?" Amber looked at his body and couldn't help but imagine what climaxes he could bring her to.

"I would love to show you." Trevor's words rolled off his tongue. His cell phone began to ring before he could continue his seductive slew of words. He saw the caller ID and pressed the IGNORE button.

"Are you sure you don't want to get that?" Amber asked, noticing the sudden change in his demeanor.

"Nah, I'm good. Just an annoying bug, if you know what I mean." His phone rang again. This time he answered it in a low, stern voice. "I told you I will talk to you after I get off work. Now, stop fucking calling me."

"Sounds like you need a break to handle some private matters. Maybe we should put a hold on that wining and dining me," said Amber, trying to make light of the situation.

Trevor's phone began to ring again. He looked at the caller ID and answered it with a grin. "My man, can I call you back in five?" Trevor held his hand up to prevent Amber from walking away.

Amber rolled her eyes and walked away, but she was interested in who Trevor was so angry with. She knew he had no kids, and didn't think he had a steady girlfriend. She definitely didn't want to get involved in any love triangle.

***

It was already twelve-thirty, and her stomach was crying for nourishment. She walked out of her office and headed for her car. The country club was only a mile and a half away, but she wanted to be there before her father and their newly appointed employee.

Amber entered the country club and headed for the dining area. The staff knew her and her father well. She was seated out on the balcony, at her favorite table overlooking the pool. She quickly placed her order with the waiter and waited for her father.

When her lunch arrived, so did her father, with a shockingly handsome, tall, caramel-toned, slender man at his side. Amber sat up straight and knew she couldn't gobble down her lunch, as she had planned.

"Hello, Daddy." Amber stood to kiss her father on the cheek.

"Hello, sweetie. Amber, I would like you to meet Mr. Robert Joseph Polland, Jr. He runs a car detailing business, and I would like him to handle the detailing end of our business."

"Hello, Ms. Couture. My pleasure to meet you. Your father has told me a lot about you." Robert extended his hand to shake hers.

"Please, call me Amber. I hope it was only good things." Amber chuckled lightly as she greeted her new employee and sat back down. She was instantly attracted but knew she couldn't act on it, because her father would be keeping a close eye on this new service added to his business.

"I see you have ordered lunch already. Did you order for us as well?" Ray questioned.

"No, I didn't. Sorry. But you can order lunch, and then we can get down to business." Amber glanced at Robert.

"Well, I couldn't have said it better myself." Robert smiled.

"So, Robert, let me begin by first asking, what experience have you had in the car business?" Amber asked, hoping he would have some knowledge so she wouldn't have to micromanage his every move.

"Well, honestly, Amber, I have very little, if any. When I was younger, I had an awful experience, and let's just say I told my father that this wasn't my thing." Robert sat back and waited for her response.

"So, I don't understand why you are here. If you—"

"Amber, this car business was the first business his father started, and it has been in the family for many years. Since Robert's father passed six months ago, it was natural for him to push forward and keep the family's business intact, without any delays. He is the oldest, and if I remember correctly, Robert, your mom knows everything about how this operation is held together. Am I correct about that?" Ray interjected.

"Absolutely correct, Ray. My mother's years of watching, listening, and traveling with my father taught her everything there is to know about the business. So, I figured, why not get a crash course from my mother and move ahead? Besides, my father wanted it this way." Robert smiled at Ray.

"Okay, but it's not just washing cars, I hope you know. You can't just say you know what a car looks like and know how to clean it. Some of our clients have special paints, secret compartments, a certain way they want their cars waxed. I just can't see how you can have a crash course on that and run a professional detailing business." Amber's tone was full of irritation at this point.

"Amber, now, honey, let's calm down a little. Robert is here. I have known his family for years, and like his father helped me at one time, I am here to help him. And, you know for a fact that the more we help our own, the better. That will be the only way we can grow. Now, since we cleared that up, let's talk some numbers, and you two can handle all the details of the day-to-day operations at another time." Ray spoke quickly, not wanting any details of his interactions with Robert's family to be exposed. Ray's eyes alerted Robert not to mention any of his dealings with his father to Amber.

Their lunch lasted over three hours. Amber learned she was now in charge of overseeing Robert, who would detail all the cars on the lot every other week and would handle clients that came in for repairs or service on a daily basis. She couldn't believe her father was getting into a business relationship with someone that was new to the car business. Her father had a soft heart when it came to black-owned businesses. He had always believed if you helped your own, it would always bring a prosperous outcome, even if it meant giving an opportunity on a silver platter. She loved that about her father.

Ray Couture was the type of man that would bend over backward to help someone out, especially an employee, if they deserved it. Trevor was one of those employees. Trevor came from a broken home and was involved in some criminal activity before he was employed at her father's dealership. Ray never discussed Trevor's background with his daughter but insisted she supervise his work.

After the lunch meeting was over, Amber gave Robert all her contact information and scheduled a 10:00 A.M. meeting for the next day. She headed out of the country club to her car. She couldn't help herself when she stopped at McDonald's for a Big Mac and fries on her way back to the office. Ever since Amber hit puberty, her weight had always been on the heavier side. After being teased in elementary school for her size, she made a dramatic change over the summer before she entered high school. Amber didn't want to be tortured by others about her weight during her years of high school. She wanted everyone to look at her when she walked into a room, and she definitely wanted as many boys as possible to want her attention. Amber worked out four hours a day every day that summer and ate only vegetarian meals. By the time the first day of high school came around, Amber was well-toned and thick. Her body was the shape of a grown woman in her early twenties.

She arrived at her office, feeling stuffed and guilty. Amber was trying to lose weight but always cheated on any diet she was on. She had talked herself into joining a gym but rarely went. If she did go to the gym, she wouldn't stay for long. She felt as though all the men were watching her and the women were laughing at her.

Amber's self-consciousness always got the better of her.

Her cell phone began to ring as she sat at her desk. "Hello, baby. How's your day going?" Amber said with a smile.

"It's going well. How about yours?" Stephen asked.

"Oh, I am wrapping it up here. I had a long lunch meeting with Dad today. Are you joining me for dinner tonight?"

"Ummm . . . sorry, honey, but I have a potential investor that needs to be wined and dined tonight. But I can stop by afterward for dessert." Stephen laughed.

"Dessert, huh? Well, you sure can. After all, it's been a while. I am beginning to think you have someone else feeding your sweet tooth," Amber said with a little disappointment.

"You are the only one that can satisfy my sweet tooth."

"Since I have you on the phone, I wanted to talk to you about making another investment. Do you think if I invest another fifty thousand, I can double the rate of return on my investment within the next six months? I can cut you the check tonight, when I see you," Amber said with excitement.

"Baby, are you sure? I mean, you can. It's a great time to do it. There are mergers with some huge technology companies in the works as we speak. Do you think your father would like to invest as well?" Stephen questioned, hoping for the right answer.

"That sounds good, but you know my dad. He won't invest, because we're dating. You know how he feels about mixing business and pleasure. That's why I haven't said a word to him. I'm waiting for a return check so I can show him how much money he can make. By the way, when do you think I will get that check, since my first investment was six months ago?" Amber asked with a little concern in her voice.

"Ummm . . . we will talk about that tonight, okay? I have to go. A client from Japan is on the other line. See you later." Stephen quickly ended the conversation.

"Steph . . ." Amber was cut short and was now listening to a dial tone.

Damn. Oh well, I guess it's an important call. I will have to talk to him tonight about that check, Amber thought to herself.

She logged off her computer and shut it down. Amber noticed Trevor watching her. She removed her blazer so he could see her double Ds better. He licked his lips as he watched her move around her office. Amber loved to see men salivate over her, especially those without a chance. *Those skinny bitches have nothing on me. I can still get whoever I want, no matter how big I am.* Amber smiled, thinking of all the men that wanted her.

Chapter 2

Stephen sat at Il Gabbiano on South Biscayne Boulevard and looked at his Rolex. It was now nine o'clock. He had been waiting for over thirty minutes. He waved the waitress over.

"Yes, sir? Can I get anything for you?" the waitress asked.

"Yes, I am expecting someone else to arrive and was wondering if you can inquire with the hostess if my guest has arrived." Stephen reached for his phone on the table and texted, Where are you? You're late.

"I'm right here," a sexy voice whispered behind him.

Stephen smiled with glee as he stood to hug this beautiful, green-eyed, blonde bombshell. She stood five foot six inches with heels, and her well-toned Coke bottle figure had all eyes on her. He called her Candy because her body was so sweet.

"Candy, my love, thank you for gracing me with your presence." Stephen kissed her full lips.

"Sorry I'm late. I had an unexpected photo shoot I had to get done," Candy nonchalantly said.

"I thought you were all finished with that."

"Yes, but one of the clubs I work for called me, and they wanted me to do some test shots at the reopening of Playmates Club. Well, it used to be called Alleycat. I hope they will put me on the cover again." Candy crossed her fingers.

"They would be stupid not to. Would you like some champagne to celebrate, then?" Stephen held her hand in his and signaled the waitress to come over.

"Yes, sir? Are you ready to order?" the waitress asked.

"Can I have a bottle of Krug Clos du Mesnil, nineteen ninety-five?" Stephen said with ease.

"Sir, I will check to see if we have any in stock. We rarely get such a request. Please, give me a minute or two." The waitress was a bit blown back at his expensive taste, but she knew fulfilling his request would be well rewarded.

The waitress arrived within minutes with his bottle of champagne, along with the manager.

"Sir, you have requested one of the best champagnes in the world. I just had to meet you. My name is Giovanni. I am the executive manager here." He extended his hand to shake Stephen's.

"Nice to meet you, Giovanni. My name is Stephen."

"Can I have the pleasure of having our chef put together a delicious meal for you and your lovely guest?" Giovanni asked, sensing a piercing eye from the waitress.

Stephen turned to Candy. "Are you okay with that, Candy?"

"Sure. Why not? But I am allergic to seafood." Candy looked to Giovanni.

"No problem. Sir, are you allergic to anything as well?"

"Yes, basil. Will that be a problem?" Stephen asked with a grin.

"No, sir, not at all. Your waitress will be back to serve you the first of four courses."

"Thank you, Giovanni. Again, it was great to meet you." Stephen reached into his pocket and discreetly slipped him a crisp one-hundred-dollar bill.

Giovanni gladly accepted and rushed to the kitchen.

Candy tilted her head to the side. "Stephen, since when are you allergic to anything?"

Stephen laughed as he raised his glass to toast. "I'm not, but if this place is as good as they say, then the chef shouldn't have a problem. *Buona fortuna!*"

"Good luck, indeed." Candy sipped her champagne. "Wow, this is good."

"Well, it better be for two thousand dollars."

Candy's eyes widened. "Damn, I guess I am special."

"Sweetness, you will always be special to me." Stephen retrieved a small black velvet box from the inside pocket of his blazer. He placed the box on the table and opened it.

Candy sat perfectly still. She was stunned by the flawless three-carat diamond studs he presented to her. Her jaw dropped.

"Do you not like them? I picked them just for you."

"I love them." Candy immediately left her seat to hug and kiss Stephen. "I just love them. . . . Thank you, thank you. Stephen, you are the best boyfriend I have ever had."

Stephen and Candy sat with each other for another two hours, while their courses of food were served continually. Their waitress didn't skip a beat. As soon as they finished one course, another was placed in front of them. When the last course was served, they noticed they were the only ones left dining and the entire staff was now there to serve them.

Stephen's cell phone rang. He looked at the caller ID and ignored the call. Candy excused herself to go to the ladies' room, and he signaled the waitress for the bill. A few seconds later his phone rang again, but this time he answered it, since Candy wasn't in earshot. "Hey, baby. I'm on my way. I just finished getting another investor."

"Stephen, it's almost midnight. Your dessert is waiting for you," Amber purred into the phone.

"Sorry, honey. We got kind of got carried away with celebrating. I will be there in an hour. Okay?"

"I have that sexy lingerie on that you brought me, with your favorite pair of red bottom stilettos."

"Oh, yeah . . . I guess I will be running those red lights to get there. See you soon." Stephen pressed the END button.

Candy returned, yawning before sitting down. "Who were you talking to at this late hour?"

"Oh, a client from Poland. He always gets the time screwed up. Are you ready to go? I will take you home, but I can't stay. I have an early day tomorrow."

"Okay, I guess I will have to thank you another time." Candy giggled.

"Oh, no, you can still thank me. We have a twenty-minute drive to your house." Stephen's grin made her giggle even more.

"Okay, pay the bill and let's go." Candy reached into her purse and took out her lipstick to apply a fresh coat to her full lips.

Stephen left fifteen hundred dollars on the table and headed for the door, wishing Giovanni and the staff a good night. The anticipation of Candy's lips on his manhood made it rise, making his step a little faster toward the car. Stephen unzipped his trousers as soon as he sat in the driver's seat. Candy's wet lips and tight grip on his stiff wood made him moan as he drove away from the restaurant. Her sucking and jerking made him veer to the left twice and almost hit the median strip. Luckily, there weren't a lot of cars on the highway. Needless to say, he was a happy camper when they arrived at the gated entrance to her complex. After driving into the complex, he headed to her building to let her out.

"Thank you, baby. Will I see you later on today so I can properly thank you?" Candy asked as she retrieved some tissue out of her purse to wipe her lips.

"If that wasn't a proper thank-you, then I will definitely see you later to get my proper thank-you." Stephen kissed her passionately, then unlocked the doors to the car.

Candy couldn't help but laugh at his statement. "I bet I will see you later." Candy stepped out of the car and entered her building.

"Please, baby, don't cum yet. . . . We can do so much more. . . . Please, don't . . . ," Amber whispered in Stephen's ear as she rocked back and forth on his solid wood.

"Oh . . . oh . . . damn . . . I can't hold back. . . . I'm cumming, baby. . . . Don't stop. . . . Yes . . . yes . . . ahhhhh . . ." Stephen released with pleasure.

Amber noticed that what was once stiff and hard inside her was now as limp and lifeless as a noodle. She felt it slowly slipping out of her flesh. Her disappointment was a bigger hit when she glanced at the clock. *Fucking ten minutes. What the fuck is his problem? If this continues, I will have to get someone to fulfill my needs. Fuck.* Amber's thoughts were interrupted by Stephen's gesture for her to get off of him.

"Is everything okay?" Amber asked.

"Yeah, that was good, baby. Just what I needed. Was it not good for you?" Stephen gently kissed her lips.

"Of course . . . yes, just what I needed, too. Are you ready for another round?" Amber held her breath, hoping he would say yes.

"I can't. I have an early day tomorrow. I'm going to take a shower and get ready for bed. It's already two in the morning."

"Oh, okay. Well, then next time don't arrive so late," Amber said with an attitude.

"Listen, I could have not come at all. My meeting didn't end till midnight. You know what? Maybe I better get dressed and head to my own place," Stephen said, not in the mood for her arguing.

"If you feel that way, then by all means see yourself out." Amber got off the bed and headed into her master bathroom and closed the door behind her. She was pissed off after waiting all evening for only ten minutes of semi-pleasure. She wanted more.

Amber stepped into the shower and turned the water on. She let the warm water hit her body while she stood in thought. *I think I just fucked up everything. This is the right man for me. He can take care of me. My dad adores him. He's faithful to me, or so he says. Quick note to self. Need a private investigator to make sure. It's just sex. I can get toys to satisfy me, or we can go to a sex therapist to help us. Oh, my God, I can't lose him. He's the only man I have allowed to get this close to me and have kept around this long.*

Amber quickly stepped out of the shower, toweled off, and opened her bathroom door. She was surprised to see Stephen drifting off to sleep in her bed. She quietly got in bed and lay next to him, whispering, "I'm sorry, baby. I just want more time with you."

He opened his eyes and turned to her. "It's okay. We will work it out." Stephen kissed her lips and pulled her naked body closer to him. They both drifted off to sleep.

Amber awoke the next morning to breakfast in bed. "Oh, baby, you didn't have to do this. . . ."

"No, I did. I don't like it when you are mad at me, and besides, you need to start your day off right. I made some blueberry pancakes, bacon, with one slice of whole wheat toast, and of course, your latte," Stephen said, hoping this would smooth everything out.

"This is perfect. Aren't you going to join me?"

"No, I can't. I have an early meeting this morning, but I will pick you up for lunch around noon. Is that okay?" Stephen asked.

"Yeah, that will be great. So, are you mad at me about last night?" Amber asked, reaching for her coffee on the tray on her nightstand.

"No, not at all. I know we have been spending less time together, but you have to understand I have all these hedge-fund investors that take up most of my time. But now that I know you are serious with me, I will do my best to spend all of my free time with you. How does that sound?"

"Serious with you? We . . . we have been seeing each other for the past eight months. You have met my father, and you two even go golfing together on a regular basis. Now, if that's not serious, then what are we?" Amber said loudly.

"Amber, I'm not trying to get into an argument with you about how serious we are. I love you, and honestly, I don't think I can live without you." Stephen took her coffee out of her hand and placed it on the nightstand. He grabbed her and kissed her feverishly. He gently played with her nipples, making them salute within seconds. He removed his boxers in one swift motion and buried his head between her legs, licking her clit and slowly moving his finger in and out of her peach.

"Ahh . . . baby . . ." Amber cooed.

"It tastes so good. . . ." Stephen sucked on her rapidly, wanting her to explode.

"Don't stop. . . . It feels so good. . . ."

Stephen kept up his vigorous speed with his tongue and waited for her to climax. He entered her on cue. He stroked her deep and hard, just the way she liked it, until she peaked again.

Stephen collapsed, out of breath, beside Amber. "How was that wake-up call?"

"Oh, baby, please wake me up like that more often," Amber said, smiling from ear to ear.

Stephen laughed, almost choking on his saliva. *I hope this is the perfect time to ask for that check,* Stephen thought. "Amber, are you still going to write that check?"

"After that I might just write it for a hundred thousand." Amber laughed while easing herself off the bed. She walked over to her desk and retrieved her checkbook from the top drawer.

"Now, remember, baby, you are the only client of mine that gets that special treatment."

Amber wrote the check for sixty thousand dollars and placed it in her mouth. She walked to the bed, where Stephen was still lying, and climbed slowly onto it. She playfully moved away when he tried to grab the check. He removed the sheets that covered his body and put his hands in the air, giving her a mischievous look. Amber knew what he wanted and quickly spit the check on the bed, then lowered her head to devour his manhood in her mouth.

Stephen reached for the check on the bed and used his other hand to guide the movement of her head. The feeling of a wet, warm mouth wasn't the only pleasure he was receiving. He held the check tightly in his hand. *I need to make this quick so I can get out of here.* Stephen closed his eyes, thinking of his Candy.

Chapter 3

Amber drove to her office, still on a high from her wake-up call. *Now, why can't it be like that all the time? Well, I guess once in a while is better than never.* She arrived at her office and greeted everyone with smiles. She even ordered coffee and breakfast for all the employees. She settled into her office with fifteen minutes to spare before her meeting with Robert.

"Excuse me, Ms. Couture. . . ." Trevor entered her office.

Amber looked up to see him standing in front of her in a tan tank top that showed his luscious biceps. "Yes, Mr. Turner, how can I help you? You did get the part for the BMW Six Series Coupé, correct?"

"Oh yes, but I actually just wanted to personally thank you for the coffee and breakfast this morning," Trevor said with a smile on his face.

"Oh, you're welcome. No big thing. I'm in a good mood, so don't do anything to spoil it,"

Amber said as she logged on to her computer with a smile.

"So do you think—" Trevor was abruptly interrupted by a knock on the door.

"Good morning, Amber. I hope I am not too early for our meeting. You did say ten, right?" Robert entered her office and looked at Trevor. He thought he knew him from the old neighborhood.

Amber looked at her watch. "Right on time. Please have a seat." Amber turned to Trevor. "I'm sorry, Trevor, but can we continue this later?"

"Oh, yeah, no problem. Again thanks." Trevor quickly left.

Robert watched Trevor as he left. "Is that one of your employees? I think I know his face."

"Yes, that's Trevor Turner, one of our top mechanics. He's been working here for about two years now. If I am correct, he's from the same neighborhood as you."

"Yes, he looks extremely familiar, but I just can't place him," Robert said, reaching for his briefcase. "Okay, so I have a schedule for you to look over and approve. This is based on the information you sent after our initial meeting." Robert handed her a spreadsheet.

Amber placed the spreadsheet in front of her. "Yes, I like it, but you have no room to spare for some of our emergency clients. Can we adjust some of this?"

"Yes, of course. Please, go right ahead."

Amber grabbed a pencil and adjusted some time frames. "Okay, I know it cuts your time down, but I am sure you can get it done. I see you have only two guys working on each car. . . . Do you think we can have three or four guys working on each car? That way, if an emergency client does happen to show up, we can just bump a couple of guys and accommodate the client."

"Of course. So we can have your service clients' cars done without losing any time, if they want it." Robert looked around her office and spotted a picture of a young, white, tall, dark-haired man behind her, with piercing blue-green eyes. He wanted to ask if he was her boyfriend, but opted for keeping his mouth shut.

"So, I think we have an airtight schedule with some room to move stuff around. I think we are done here. I will e-mail you every morning our client schedule for the day and will leave you to handle the rest. Sounds good?" Amber handed him the revised spreadsheet.

Robert looked at the spreadsheet. "Okay, so since you have only four clients today, we are going to have to rearrange some guys. My guys have already started detailing the cars out back that your dad had ready for some clients. Would you like to check it out?"

"I sure would, and I can give you a tour as well." Amber rose from her seat.

"No need for the tour. Your father provided me with that this morning. Actually, I have been here since six," Robert said, smiling.

"Oh, okay." Amber blushed with slight embarrassment. "Well, you should know"—she placed her fingers on her lips and paused—"I'm never here before ten . . ." Amber said, walking out of her office, with Robert following closely behind.

"So, Robert, since we will be working with each other, tell me about yourself." Amber fished for some details that her father didn't provide.

"Well, I like all types of music, and I love to sing. I love movie comedies, and I do like to eat." Robert walked slowly alongside Amber, hanging on her every word.

"Yeah, my dad did mention that our fathers did some business together a while back. He has been looking for a new detailer since the last company scratched the first Maserati we had on the lot." Amber sucked her teeth, remembering the incident.

"I bet your father was pissed."

"*Pissed* is not the word. He fired them on the spot and demanded they pay for the repair. Ever since then, we've been bouncing back and forth between local detailers." Amber stood outside, watching the care the detailers took with the 2011 Rolls-Royce Ghost.

"I'm happy that your father has given me this opportunity. Hopefully, I won't let him or you down." Robert turned to Amber and flashed a smile.

"Well, from what I see here, I don't think we will have a problem. I guess I was a little hard on you before. And I'm sure your mother provided you with the essential details of the business." Amber flashed her pearly whites.

Robert stared at Amber, lost in her beauty. His mind wondered if he could take her out on a date. "Robert, is everything okay?" Amber asked, noticing his minor daze.

"Oh, I'm sorry. Yes, I'm sure we won't have a problem. Do you think you could school me on a few things about the cars?" Robert asked, wanting more time with her.

"Sure, anytime. We can do lunch or something, but not today. I have a previous engagement," Amber replied.

"No problem. I hope we can get to know each other a little better." Robert smiled.

"I am sure we will. After all, you've got something to prove to me," Amber said.

"Oh, really? So, you still don't believe I can do this, huh?" Robert stood with his arms folded.

"Actually, I dare you to do this and do it well. No, not just well, but outstandingly," Amber said.

"Well, I guess I better get back to work before you put me in a slacker category," Robert joked.

Amber winked and walked back to her office, laughing to herself. It was only eleven o'clock, so she decided to call Stephen to confirm their lunch date that afternoon. Before she could dial his phone number, it appeared on her caller ID.

"Hello, baby."

"Hey, sweetheart. How's your morning going?" Stephen asked, pretending to care.

"Well, it's much better now that I am talking to you." Amber spoke softly, with a slight giggle.

"Oh, really . . . umm, baby . . ."

"That doesn't sound good," Amber said with disappointment in her voice.

"I have an important meeting with a client, and I have to cancel lunch, but we can meet later for dinner, around eight. I'm truly sorry, baby, but this meeting is extremely important," Stephen stated.

"Well, it better be. I guess I will just have to wait," said Amber.

"Don't the best things come to those who wait?"

"Yes, they do, but I was so looking forward to seeing you sooner rather than later. That's all."

Stephen heard the displeasure in her voice. "I have a surprise for you, and I think you will just love it."

Amber perked up and was smiling once again. "Great. You know I love your gifts."

"Then, it's settled. I will see you around eight. Amber . . ."

"Yes, Stephen? I'm still here."

"I love you. See you later, my darling."

"Yes, I can't wait. Oh, and, Stephen, I love you, too." Amber hung up the phone with excitement and love on her mind.

After the phone call, she was back on her cloud nine. She wondered if her gift was a custom fit or a knockoff. *Damn, could this be the four-carat solitaire diamond ring I have looked at every time he has taken me jewelry shopping for the last month?* She smiled at the thought.

Her daydream was quickly interrupted by a knock at her door. It was Trevor.

"I wish I could make you smile like that . . . ," Trevor said seductively.

His voice instantly made her panties moist. "Who knows? Maybe you can." Her sultry tone broadcast her interest loud and clear.

He entered her office and closed the door behind him. He stood there, shocked that after all his work, she was actually showing him some love. *So she's not a cold bitch, after all,* he thought as he took a seat in front of her desk. "You serious? Don't play with me." He sat back, with his arms folded, and stared at her.

Amber stood watching the garage through her glass entrance and then walked to the front of her desk. She extended her legs as she sat on the edge of her desk. "Now, Mr. Turner, you know you can always put a smile on my face. You know it will never work out. We have nothing in common, so"—she stood and walked back behind her desk—"Mr. Turner, if you don't mind, I gotta get some work done." She smiled as she took her seat and turned her eyes toward the door.

"Oh, okay . . . I guess you just want to continue the charades." Trevor stood up and walked out.

Amber didn't want him to feel too comfortable. She wanted him on her terms only. She looked at the time on her computer. *Almost one o'clock. I think it's time for some lunch and maybe a little bit of shopping for my date tonight,* she thought. But before she grabbed her purse to head out, she suddenly stopped and her smile disappeared. She sat at her desk, thinking. *Damn, well, I better do it before I regret it,* she thought as she skimmed through her Rolodex.

"Hey, I have a job for you. Do you think you can meet me at our regular spot in thirty?" she said into the phone.

"Yes," a strong, deep voice answered.

"Great. See you there." Amber hung the phone up and stood up, but before walking out, she grabbed the picture of her and Stephen. *You better be who I think you are.* She plucked his face in the picture. She removed the picture from the frame and placed it in an envelope. She took the envelope and her purse and headed out the door for her meeting. A meeting that she hoped would be uneventful, but only time would tell.

Amber arrived with two minutes to spare. She scanned the room quickly and noticed that he was already there. *Damn, no matter where he's at, he always seems to get here before me or my father,* she thought. But what could you expect? He was an ex-agent from the CIA.

"Hey, I am starving. I see you have already ordered." Amber inhaled the smell of meat and hurried into her seat at the sight of the food. "Nothing like a good steak. Thanks."

"So, what's my job? Another employee background check?" He continued eating, without even looking at her or greeting her.

"No, but that's a good idea." She quickly put a piece of steak into her mouth.

"Look, like I told your father, I don't mind doing this if the price is right, but this has no action, and I need that excitement to continue to do this." He spoke to her as if she were a child.

Amber stopped eating and looked at him. "Please, don't disrespect me with your tone. This is business. Now, if you don't want the ten grand, then, please, be my guest and exit."

The ex-agent stopped eating and looked at her. "Yes, you are right. This is business. Let's get down to it. First, this will cost you twenty grand, and second, I need ten now." He smirked.

Amber knew exactly what kind of power game he was playing, but she didn't want to cause any friction between him and her father. She knew if this was going to stay between them, she would have to pay the price he demanded. If her father found out that she had any doubts about Stephen, he would refuse to make any business investments and to cultivate the friendship, immediately. She reached for her purse and retrieved the envelope. She handed it to him and said, "Find everything you can on him. His name is Stephen

Hunter. He's a hedge-fund broker. I need to know where he goes, who he sees. . . ."

"I know the questions. Give me a week. Now, just give me my ten, and I will call you then." He stuffed the envelope into his jacket pocket.

"Give me two minutes." Amber reached for her iPad in her purse. "You bank Swiss, correct?"

"Yes."

Amber pulled up her account and set up the transfer and then handed the iPad to him. "Tap your account number in and hit send."

He did what he was told. He tucked the iPad under his arm and stood to walk out.

"Excuse me. Aren't you forgetting something?" Amber asked, annoyed.

"Our business has concluded. Am I not correct?" He spoke with a smile.

"Excuse me, but where do you think you're going with my iPad?"

"Oh, this?" He took the iPad out from under his arm and showed it to her. "This is mine now. You didn't actually think I was just going to tap my account in and hand it back to you? I know what I can do with an account number." He laughed.

"Yeah, I get it, but what about my stuff on there? I got work shi—"

"Whatever you got here will be sent to you on a brand-new iPad by the time you return to the office. Fair?" He laughed at her statement.

"One thing. Since it will be an entirely new one, then please send me the upgrade. I was planning to get it today, but this will have saved me the hassle. Thanks." She stabbed a piece of steak and stuck it into her mouth.

He laughed as he walked out.

Amber couldn't help but smile, because a brand-new iPad 2 would be at her office in a few hours and she would know in a week if Stephen was who he said he was. Amber waved the waitress over and ordered a martini to celebrate.

Chapter 4

After shopping at Nordstrom for the perfect cocktail dress, Manolo Blahnik shoes, and a handbag, Amber looked at her watch, saw two hours had passed, and cursed herself for taking so long. *Damn it, Amber! You are supposed to be an executive and to set examples for your employees' behavior. Shit, shit, shit!* Amber hurried the saleswoman. She reached for her wallet and pulled out her AmEx and almost threw it at her.

"I'm so sorry. . . . I didn't mean that. I'm just in a rush," Amber said with her most sincere voice. She reached into her wallet again and pulled out two one-hundred-dollar bills and discreetly handed them to her.

The saleswoman looked at the money and started to move at lightning speed, cutting out all the spiel about her purchases and the return policies. Amber smiled, signed her credit card receipt, grabbed her bags, and headed toward the exit.

Amber walked out of the mall with speed, heading to her car in the parking lot. When she was close enough, she popped the trunk and practically threw her bags in before it had even opened entirely. She opened the car door, hopped into the driver's seat, and raced off to her office. She loved the benefits of her job, but as an executive, she always thought taking advantage of those privileges showed that you were a little too comfortable. She'd always told her employees that everyone was replaceable, including herself.

She reached the dealership in record time, pulled into her parking spot, and almost drove through the glass showroom. She put her car in park and took a deep breath. "Amber, slow the fuck down!" she muttered to herself. She closed her eyes, counted to ten, then grabbed her purse off the passenger's seat and rushed out of the car. Amber looked at her watch. *Damn, I only got an hour to finish all my shit. I guess I will just have to get that shit done. No distractions,* she thought as she scurried to her office.

Amber zipped past Trevor, not noticing their near collision.

Trevor saw only her voluminous ass, and her scent of jasmine lingered lightly. "Damn, Ms. Couture, you almost went through me," he said in a low tone. *I'm going to get her today. Fuck that! It's that money I'm after, nothing else.*

It's got to happen today. He rubbed his chin in thought. Trevor wanted this to go smooth, and his first-time performance would have to be his best. His phone vibrated in his pocket. He looked at the new text message.

I'm not sure about this. I don't think I can live with this.

Trevor quickly replied:

Look, it don't matter what u say. It's a done deal. I see you already made up your mind. So you give me no choice but to live with it. You better make sure your first purchase has to do with me. One.

Trevor smiled. *This is gonna be good. I'm ready to blow this joint, anyway. My probation will end soon.*

Amber rushed to her desk and noticed a small box. She opened it, and it was a brand-new iPad 2. She knew her computer would be replaced, just not that quickly. *Well, I guess I am getting my own respect,* she thought. Amber didn't have time to play with her new toy, and she quickly got to work. She tried not to peek at Trevor but couldn't help stealing glances every so often. Before she knew it, the digital clock on her computer read 6:07 P.M. She hurried to wrap it up so she could be home in time to shower and get dressed for her eight o'clock date with Stephen.

Trevor lingered around, working slowly to ensure privacy. He waited 'til the last person had left the garage, and headed toward the front offices to make sure Mr. Couture wasn't around, or any other execs, for that matter. If he wanted this to work, he had to make sure it was safe for her as well. He headed back toward the garage after assuring himself that the coast was clear. Before he walked to Amber's office, he got some nervous laughter out of his system.

A knock sounded on the door.

Amber looked up and saw Trevor standing there in a fitted pair of blue jeans and a new white tank top, with his T-shirt hanging over his shoulder. Her heart started to beat a little faster, and a slight perspiration started to form on her brow.

"You gonna stay here all night?" Trevor finally said, walking closer to her desk.

"Nah. Actually, I am wrapping it up and heading out the door myself. You smell good. What cologne is that?" Amber started to reach for her purse, but Trevor grabbed it for her. Their bodies were close to touching. Amber inched back slowly and looked around.

"Nah, ain't nobody here but us. So what charade you want to play now?" Trevor gently glided his fingers down her arms.

Amber immediately felt goose bumps appear. She stepped closer. This time her hard nipples rubbed against his chest. "Trevor, what if this is all I want, and nothing else? Would you be willing to go with that?"

"Oh, but the question is, are *you* going to be good with that?" Trevor asked, reaching for her thighs.

"No, I can't do this. What am I doing? You work for my family. I don't sleep with the help," Amber said playfully, slapping his hand away and stepping away.

"So, is that what you really want?" Trevor flexed his chest muscles. "I know you want it. You just too scared to come get it." He inched a little closer and tried to kiss her.

Amber moved her head, slowly pretending to fight the urge to ram her tongue down his throat. All she could think of was his body rocking on her body. She hadn't gotten what she liked in quite some time and definitely wanted her aggressions worked out. Besides, she figured Trevor wouldn't work there for long, anyway, once she got fed up with her plaything.

Trevor saw the hesitation and stepped back. "What is it? Is it 'cause I'm not one of your little rich boyfriends? Baby, I am gonna show you that material ain't the only thing that keeps a woman such as yourself."

"A woman such as me, huh? Rich little boyfriends? Are you serious? What's your name again?" Amber quickly put her hands on her hips, still struggling not to just jump on him and take advantage.

Trevor folded his arms and smiled. "Well, I really can't explain it. You know I got that poor man syndrome, not good with words. But I can tell you one thing, shorty. . . . Umm . . . excuse me. . . . I mean, Ms. Couture. . . . You can definitely use some good dick in your life."

"So, you think I am all about the money and the materialistic shit that comes with, huh? Well, let me tell you something I don't. I got my own and can get anything that I want."

"Yeah, I know that. But you know your boyfriend is white, and I know for a fact he ain't hitting that like how he should. Feel me?" Trevor grabbed at his crotch and licked his lips wet.

She sucked her teeth and turned around to walk out of the office and head home. She didn't want to acknowledge the truth about how dick hungry she really was.

Trevor quickly reached for her hand, turned her around, and his lips touched hers with as much passion as he could muster up. She didn't resist. His hands began to wander up her skirt, and to his surprise, her panties were moist. Trevor ripped her underwear off her; then he immediately took advantage and went to work on her hot spot.

"Ahh . . . no, we can't do this. . . ." Amber mumbled, allowing his tongue to play with her neck and make a wet trail to her ears.

"No one has to know, baby. Trust me, it will be our little, hot secret," he said between his lustful kisses and the swift movement of placing her on top of the desk. He parted her legs and placed two fingers deep inside her flesh.

"Mmmmm . . . please . . . stop. . . ." Amber tried to refuse, but all her smarts went right out the door. She couldn't help that his fingers felt so good. He knew exactly how to work all around her curvaceousness, and he was definitely strong.

Trevor whispered in her ear, "Do you really want me to stop?" He pushed his fingers in deeper and circled her clit with his thumb, making her moan louder.

"No . . . no . . . don't stop. . . ." Her legs started to shake. She couldn't believe how good he was.

He went in for the kill. He unbuckled his belt with his free hand and let his pants fall to his ankles.

Amber's panting became faster, letting him know she was ready for his taking.

His manhood was already making its debut through his boxers. He grabbed both her legs and placed them on his right shoulder, then slowly made his entrance into her soft, wet lips.

"Oh, yes . . . give it to me. . . . I want it. . . . Take this pussy like you want it. . . . Oh, yeah . . . fuck me!" Amber closed her eyes and happily invited his hard, deep, long thrusts, her moans and shouts echoing loudly through the office. She didn't hold back, knowing they were the only two around.

"Yeah, you like that, don't you?" Trevor spoke in a low, sexy tone as he watched her double Ds bounce up and down.

"Mmm-hmm . . . Just don't stop. . . ." She couldn't hold back on how good she felt. She closed her eyes, knowing that this was the best dick she'd had in months.

Trevor sensed that she was not getting what she needed at home. He went to work. His movements became faster and harder; then he slowed it down and watched her climax.

"Oh, yes, fuck me, baby. . . . Fuck me. . . . Give it to me . . . all of it, baby . . ." Amber screamed, pulling her legs farther back toward her head. Her yoga instructor would be proud.

"All of it . . . huh? Can you handle it?" Trevor asked as he teased her clit with his finger and pumped faster.

"Oh, yes . . . yes . . . yes . . ." Amber climaxed once again.

Trevor glanced at his watch. *Damn, it's been like forty minutes. Okay, time to pop this cherry.* He grabbed her legs and motioned for her to get off the desk and turn around. He watched her juicy, heart-shaped ass back up onto his wooden soldier. He gripped her ass tightly in his hands while his thrusts became deeper.

"Oh, fuck . . . oh, fuck . . ." Amber shouted, trying to hold on to the edge of her desk, before her legs buckled. She still wanted some control, although she'd lost it at her first climax.

"Yeah . . . yeah . . . yeah . . . ahhh . . . ," Trevor yelled as he came inside her.

Amber quickly jumped straight and pushed him off of her. "Damn, what the fuck is wrong with you?"

Trevor stood there with a screwed face after her reaction. "What the fuck you mean?"

"You never heard of pulling out?" Amber walked into the private bathroom in her office.

"Like you not on the pill or something . . ." Trevor said with a slight grin.

Amber stopped wiping herself and turned in his direction. "No, motherfucker, I'm not! Remember, I got a fucking man." She slammed the bathroom door and hoped he took the hint to leave.

Trevor pulled his boxers up and then his pants. He searched the room for his shirt. He picked it up from the floor and turned to the bathroom door. "Since you got a man, maybe you shouldn't tell him how much you enjoyed yourself. Well, I guess we can go back to playing *your* charades." He walked out of her office, leaving the door closed.

Amber's heart sank. "Damn, why did I let myself become so weak?" she said to herself in the mirror. As she opened the door to the bathroom, she heard her cell phone ring. She looked at her watch. "Oh, shit, it's eight o'clock." She hurried to her phone but couldn't find it. She searched her disheveled desk but still didn't see it. The phone stopped ringing. She searched for ten minutes and finally discovered it under her desk, alongside her ripped panties. Amber looked at her missed-call list. Not to her surprise, it had been Stephen calling. She dialed his number frantically. "Stephen, I'm so sorry."

"Is there something wrong? Why aren't you here? Did you forget that I had something special planned for you tonight?" Stephen spoke with a little attitude.

"I got caught up with work. I lost track of time, but I can be there in twenty minutes," Amber said, fumbling as she redressed.

"Well, I guess I will have to wait, then," Stephen said, annoyed by her forgetfulness.

"My spare key is under the third plant pot from the right, and the code to the alarm is zero-four-one-one. See you in a bit. I will make it up to you. I promise," Amber said as she opened her office door. She pressed END on the phone. She stepped out of her office, ran to lock up the garage, and dashed to her car.

Oh, my gosh, what have I done? The question kept swirling around in her head on the drive home.

Chapter 5

I can't believe this shit. After this I might as well keep it simple. Her lateness has already screwed up my reservations, he thought as he entered the code into the alarm. He walked into the foyer and placed the spare key on the table, next to the vase of lilies. He smelled the flowers and had an idea.

Stephen liked Amber, but not more than her money. Just three months after meeting her, he acquired twenty-five thousand dollars from her. Now that he was exclusively with her, or so she thought, his wealth was climbing. All her friends and their friends led to bigger investors. Some investments were over five figures. Stephen wanted her father to invest so he could get into the millionaires' circle of friends, but he told himself golfing would have to do for now.

He was happy with the superficial relationship he'd built with her, but wasn't too thrilled with the amount of time he spent with her. Stephen had pulled the work excuse for most of their relationship so that he didn't have to be with her all the time. He was so grateful for technology; even Facebook had helped in making Amber a prime candidate for his romance from afar. A text, a post to her wall, or just a phone call every day did wonders for a woman's heart. He took her out every so often and went to her family events just to network. He also showered her with little gifts, which kept her wanting more.

Amber sped down the expressway and made it to her house in exactly twenty minutes. She pulled into the driveway and put her car in park. Amber rushed out of the car, but when she got to the door, she remembered her outfit and shoes in the trunk. She ran back to the car to retrieve them. By the time she opened her door, sweat was dripping from her brow. She opened the door and called out Stephen's name. "Stephen, sweetie . . . where are you?"

"I'm up here," Stephen said after sipping on a glass of champagne in his hand.

"I see you have started without me." Amber smiled.

"Well, don't you look a little flushed. Hard day?" Stephen questioned, staring at her appearance.

Amber stopped and looked at herself in the full-length mirror located in the foyer. "Well, damn," Amber whispered to herself. "Well, good thing I'm home. I can jump into the shower and be ready in twenty. . . ." Amber dropped her purse to the floor and ran up the stairs to Stephen.

"Change of plans."

"Huh? Why? Okay, I can be ready in ten." Amber kissed him.

"Well, since we have missed our reservation . . . And, by the way, it cost a lot to get a table where people are waiting months for a reservation. But never mind that. We can still have a good time." Stephen brushed her hair back with his hand and grabbed her by the hand. He led her through the master bedroom into her bathroom.

Amber saw the bubble bath and melted.

"So let's get you in there . . ." Stephen said, starting to undress Amber. He removed her shirt, then her bra. He kissed her body, moving slowly to remove her skirt. He stopped abruptly. "Why is it that you have no panties on?" Stephen stepped back.

"Ummm . . . I . . ." Amber's hesitation didn't help her prevent an argument.

"Is that why you were late?" Stephen slowly walked over to the tub and shut off the water, then took a seat on the covered toilet. He bowed his head.

Amber walked over to him and placed her hand on top of his head. "Baby, my panties were bothering me, so I removed them. What makes you think I was doing something else?"

"I don't know. . . . Maybe 'cause you were late . . . and that's not like you when it comes to me . . . so it makes it different when your ass comes home with no panties!"

Stephen took this opportunity to start an argument so he could leave. He pushed her hand away from his head. "You know what? I'm going home to do some work. Enjoy your bath. Oh, yeah, your surprise is in the top drawer of the nightstand." Stephen walked past her and down the stairs to the front door.

"Stephen, please don't do this. You are making a mistake." Amber stood at the top of the staircase, fuming.

Stephen stood at the front door and then turned around. "Mistake? And what mistake would that be?" He placed his finger on his chin, as if he were thinking. "Forgetting to put your panties on after your little whatever? Fuck this. After all this time you been with me, you want to throw everything away!"

"Okay, so let me get this straight. You are leaving because I was late or because I didn't have any panties on? You know what? You are a true asshole, 'cause you know you are the only man I've been with, and you are the only one I want to be with. So, if you wanna leave, go right ahead, but just remember, I may not be here when *you* decide to return." Amber stormed into her room, grabbed the tiny box out of the nightstand. She returned to the top of the stairs to see that he had already left. She threw the box as hard as she could toward the front door.

Stephen parked in front of Candy's complex and dialed her number. "Hey, baby, would you like to take a little trip?"

"Right now? For how long?" Candy asked.

"We should be back by morning. Just come out in something spectacular, and no panties. I'm waiting." Stephen hung up the phone and dialed his private jet pilot. He spoke briefly and indicated he wanted to go to New York for the night. He said he was on his way to Miami International and he would be there in forty minutes.

Candy walked to his car, wearing an Oscar de la Renta tiny, strapless black dress. The dress hugged her body as if it were painted on. She opened the car door. "Is this good enough?"

"Yes, it is. . . . Yes, it is. . . ." Stephen smiled from ear to ear. "I hope you like the New York nightlife. There is a club called Greenhouse I want to check out."

"Fine with me, and as long as you're happy. I'm here to please you." She kissed Stephen passionately and rubbed her hand along his growing dick.

"We better save that for the plane ride. We will have two hours to spare, and besides, I think my dues are up for the Mile High Club." Stephen placed his hand on her thigh and laughed as he drove out of her complex. They headed to the airport for their departure.

Amber walked into her bathroom and looked into the mirror. "Damn, what a stupid bitch you are!" she spat at herself and turned to the shower. She turned on the hot water and got in. She let the water soothe her aching heart and swollen flesh from her earlier play session. Amber wanted to call Stephen, but she shook the thought from her mind. If she wanted to keep her man, she would have to play the game right. She made a mental note to check in with the ex-agent to see how her investigation was going.

When she finally stepped out of the shower, she dried herself off and grabbed her silk robe. Then she entered her bedroom and saw rose petals all over her bed and lit scented candles all around. She hadn't noticed them before. She felt even worse now, so she descended to the kitchen for the opened bottle of champagne—a true fix for her reckless behavior and disappointment. She heard an echoing ringing sound coming from the foyer. Maybe he fell for it, she thought, rushing to the front door.

"Damn, it's just my phone." She walked to the staircase and retrieved her phone from her purse. ROBERT POLLAND MISSED CALL was displayed on the screen. "What the fuck does he want?" She contemplated calling back and decided that she would. "Might as well call back. I got nothing else to do tonight." Amber picked up her purse and walked to her patio office with the bottle of champagne.

She dialed Robert's number. "Hey, Robert. Sorry I missed your call. I was in the shower. What's up?" She logged on to her laptop and took a seat at her desk.

"Oh, I'm sorry. Would you like to call me back?"

"No, not at all. My plans got spoiled," Amber said, still disappointed at Stephen's reaction.

"Sorry to hear that. I don't want to take too much of your time, but I was waiting for your e-mail with the client list. Do you think you can send it to me now?" Robert asked.

"I just pressed the SEND button. You should see it shortly." Amber let out a sigh.

"Ahh, yes, I have it in my in-box now." Robert sensed something was wrong. "Amber, are you okay?"

"I'm fine. Nothing a few drinks can't fix." Amber laughed.

Robert chuckled. "So, what are you drinking, if you don't mind me asking?"

"Oh, one of my favorite champagnes, Perrier-Jouët Rosé." Amber took another swig from the bottle.

"I don't think I have ever had that. . . . As you may know, I really don't know much about the finer things in life," Robert said with a little embarrassment in his voice.

"Oh, please! The finer things in life aren't always the best. What do you like to drink?"

"I actually like beer. A nice cold Heineken is my favorite." Robert smiled.

"Yes, I can definitely feel that, and don't tell me you like it with fried chicken," Amber joked.

"Oh, see you got jokes. Actually, I like it best with some steamed shrimp, crawfish, and crabs.

Something like an Old Bay–seasoned seafood boil. Have you ever had that?"

"That's my favorite, but I don't get to have it that much. My boyfriend thinks it's too much work, but I actually love the work."

Robert paused. "Well, maybe one day I can cook it for you. I better let you go. I got a schedule to organize."

Amber took another swig from the bottle. *I need the company,* she thought. "Why don't we do it together? That way you will be done in no time."

"How can I refuse help from the master organizer? Of course . . . I would like that." Robert smiled from ear to ear.

Amber was on the phone for an hour with Robert. She laughed and joked like he was an old school buddy. She just didn't know what it was, but she was comfortable with him. She could just be herself, not the person her father wanted her to be. As a young child, she was taught by her father that life was always better when you had money, and when you earned your own, there was a bigger pride within.

All she knew about Robert was that his father had just died and had left him the company. After their hour-long conversation, however, she found it rather strange that he hadn't worked in the car business with his father. She didn't want to seem nosy, but she really wanted to know why. Amber got the sense that his upbringing was far different from hers.

Chapter 6

It was six o'clock when the alarm went off. Robert turned over and hit the snooze button. He hated waking up early, but he knew that his father would be proud. Robert lay in bed and looked up at the ceiling, remembering the last conversation with his father.

"Son, I want you to learn the business and guide your siblings to the bigger picture. I know your sister and brother can be slackers at times, and your mother will need your help to keep them on the right track. So, I am asking you . . . Put your singing aside and help your mother. She can't handle it alone. You know your sister is working only until she finishes law school and your brother . . . Well, let's just be thankful he hasn't robbed us blind with his addictions. I need you, son. My days are limited, and I want to go to rest in peace knowing that everything will be all right."

"Pop, please, you know I will do anything for you and the family. I know Mom can't handle those two without backup," Robert said with sadness in his voice.

His father coughed uncontrollably. After five minutes he spoke in a slow, low tone. *"Son, I'm not saying you should give up your dream, but just put it to the side until you can find . . ."* He began to cough again.

"Take it easy, Pop. I get it. . . . Don't worry about it. . . ." He poured a cup of water for his father. A bell sounded, and his father began to grab his chest. The nurses rushed into the room. Robert stood there, watching them try to keep his father alive. He left the room to call his mother and siblings to inform them that they should come down to the hospital and say their final good-byes. His father died the next morning of respiratory failure.

"Two packs a day for twenty-five years . . . damn, Pop," Robert said out loud. He rose from the bed and walked to the bathroom to relieve himself. He turned the shower on and let the water run. He walked back into his room to turn the radio on. They were playing "Dance with My Father" by Luther Vandross, and Robert couldn't fight back the tears in his eyes as he slowly walked back into the bathroom to shower.

***

Stephen awoke ten minutes before landing on the taxiway of Miami International Airport. He looked beside him and saw Candy, naked, with only her four-inch Prada stilettos on, and soundly asleep. He began to suck on her nipples to wake her.

"Mmm . . . ," Candy moaned.

"Come on, baby. We only have about five minutes before we land . . . and I need to cum. . . ." Robert sat back on the butter leather recliner and motioned for Candy to climb on top of him.

Candy's head began to spin as she rose to accommodate her sugar daddy but lost her balance and ended up on the floor.

Stephen laughed. "I think you partied a little too hard. You want something to wake you up? A line? I still got one of those happy pills. . . ."

"Steph—"

Before Candy could finish calling his name, she puked all over the floor of the jet.

"Fuck!" Stephen shouted and rang for one of the crew members immediately.

A door slid open, and a short, young, red-haired woman stepped out. "Yes, sir? How may I help you?"

"Can you do something with this bitch and clean this shit up?" Stephen's stomach began to knot, and he himself felt like barfing. He covered his nose and walked toward the back of the jet. "When is this shit going to land? I have to get off this motherfucker . . ." he said. His muffled voice echoed.

"Sir, the plane is approaching the taxiway now. Please, have a seat. You will be off in less than sixty seconds. Your car will be waiting for you. Please, have a seat," she said with a clear, calming voice.

Stephen took a seat while he watched the red-haired woman open a cabinet and pull out an orange bag. She unzipped the bag and removed two small white sticks. She broke them in half and waved them under Candy's nose. "Okay, miss. Take it easy. Can you sit up?"

Candy shook her head and just lay on the floor.

"Sir, we have landed. You can exit now," The red-haired woman stated.

Stephen stood still and just stared at Candy on the floor, with disappointment written all over his face. He reached into his pocket for his money clip. He peeled off five one-hundred-dollar bills, crumbled them with his hand, and dropped them on her naked body. He exited the jet and told himself that Candy needed a new sugar daddy.

***

Trevor arrived early at the garage, wanting to make sure his opportunity wasn't noticeable to others. He didn't know what to expect from Amber given their close encounter the day before. He already knew that he couldn't get her pregnant. At a young age he was in a bad bicycle accident, which decreased his ability to produce live sperm.

Usually, after any act Trevor had with a woman, they were all over him the next day. He knew it would be different with Amber. He had a plan that could be a bit compromising, but he was ready to put it all in and prayed he had a straight flush. He looked around the garage and saw only one coworker there. Trevor glanced at his watch. *Shit, I only got 'bout an hour before it gets crowded,* he thought. He waited impatiently. Finally, the breakfast truck arrived. Like clockwork, his sole coworker quickly headed to the truck outside.

Okay, now is the perfect time. Let's get it poppin', Trevor's mind chimed. He looked around to make sure no one was in sight. He picked up his knapsack and hurried to Amber's office, then opened the door. Evidence of their fuck session yesterday was everywhere. Folders with invoices were scattered over the floor. He walked behind her desk and scanned it for her tissue box container. He opened his knapsack and pulled out another tissue box container, then replaced it with the one on her desk. Trevor zipped up his knapsack and headed out of the office with a smile of accomplishment on his face. He dropped his knapsack by his work area and leisurely walked to the breakfast truck. His cell phone vibrated. Trevor pulled out his phone, then read the incoming text message.

Are u done?

Trevor replied, All good. Turn it on.
Now, I just have to get those panties one more time. He smiled at the thought.

Chapter 7

Amber walked into the office around quarter to ten in the morning with her daily latte from Starbucks. She sipped her coffee, ingesting the hot liquid. She walked through the garage and saw Trevor working on a car. At that instant her mind and body felt their passion-filled interlude from the previous evening. *That's the shit that got me in trouble,* she thought as she opened the door to her office. "Oh, what the fuck," Amber mumbled under her breath, through her teeth. She walked in and closed the door, then locked it.

Amber didn't want to be reminded of what caused Stephen to leave her, and she definitely didn't want her father to walk in and see her office in such disarray. She started to pick up all the folders and papers on the floor. She came across her torn panties, covered by some papers under her desk. She picked them up and quickly threw them in the garbage.

After cleaning her office, she sat at her desk and logged in to her computer. She reached for her cell phone but got interrupted by a knock at her door. "Come in," she said, forgetting that the door was locked.

There was another knock at the door, and this time a familiar voice called her name. "Amber . . . is everything okay?"

"Oh, one moment . . ." Amber quickly jumped up to unlock the door. She looked around to make sure nothing was out of place. "Good morning, Daddy. How are you?"

"I think the question is, are you okay? Since when did you start locking doors? Is there something I should be aware of?" Ray Couture questioned with concern.

"Daddy, I'm a big girl now. I must have locked it by accident. I'm fine. There's nothing wrong. What's up?" Amber smiled and motioned for her father to have a seat.

"Just wanted an update on our detailing department."

"Oh, Daddy, come on. *Detailing department* . . ." Amber chuckled. "I love how you are able to make something small sound so big. And I guess Robert is"—Amber tried to fight her laughter—"the chief executive of this department, huh?"

"Ha-ha. Haven't I taught you that when you're given a title, your prestige and self-confidence become more effective, for the company's benefit. So, Ms. Vice President, let me ask you again. How is our detailing department looking?" Ray smiled.

"Funny . . . Too bad that title shit don't work on me." She turned to her computer and typed. "Let's see. . . . Actually, everything is on the up-and-up. I have gotten some good feedback from our clients as well. So, everything is good with our chief executive. . . ." Amber laughed.

"Okay. Then I guess if there aren't any other issues, I can conclude this business meeting." Ray rose from his seat and headed to the door.

"Dad, there is one thing. . . . Can you tell me why you hired Trevor?" Amber asked.

"Is there a problem with him?" Ray asked with a serious face.

"Well, I know how much you like his work. . . . And don't get me wrong, he is one of our best, but . . . I have noticed some lateness and minor equipment missing . . . and . . ." Amber dropped some hints about wanting Trevor to be fired.

"Okay, I don't think I can keep it from you any longer." Ray stood up and walked over to close the door. "The deal with Trevor is that me and his father were great friends at one time, and he begged me to bring him over here from New York and give him a job. He wanted his only son to live to see his twenty-second birthday. Trevor was in some trouble with not going to school, drug dealing, gang affiliations, and even involvement with stolen cars, so—"

"What the fuck? Stolen cars! Dad, are you serious?" Amber stood and began to pace the floor of her office.

"Honey, everything has been fine up until now. . . . I mean, you did say that he was slacking and there has been some missing equipment, right? Listen, he has been here working and not getting into any trouble for the past two years, and now that his probation is finished at the end of the week, he knows that he can either stay or go. I will have one of the security guards look through the surveillance footage and see if we have a problem. For now I want you just to keep cool and calm. I will have a talk with him later on today to make sure things are right . . . because you know there's nothing worse than being fucked by someone who's benefited off you." Ray walked over to his daughter and gave her a gentle kiss on her forehead, assuring her everything would be fine.

Amber hugged her father tightly. "Okay, Dad. You will handle it . . . I guess. . . ."

"Yes, I will handle everything. You just continue to do what you do, darling. Oh, yeah, I have been meaning to ask you how Stephen and you are doing."

"Oh, that. It's . . . going . . ." Amber quickly took a seat in front of her computer.

"Is there trouble in the love nest?" Ray seated himself.

"Why? Has he said anything to you? Don't you two play golf every week?" Amber snapped.

"Honey, I didn't mean to hit a nerve. And, no, he hasn't said anything to me, nor have I seen him for the past two weeks. I'm sure he's just busy. You know he's been working hard since you two have been dating. Maybe you guys should take a vacation together. . . . I'm sure that's all you guys need." Ray stood, not wanting to meddle in his daughter's love life.

"Yeah . . . maybe that's what we need. . . ." Amber looked at her phone.

"Okay, well, just let me know when you plan on going. . . ." Ray smiled and walked out of his daughter's office.

Amber picked up her phone and dialed Stephen's number but quickly hung up, not wanting to upset him if he was in the middle of something. She decided on sending him a text.

Hey, baby. Are u still mad? I miss u. Can u call me when you have some time to spare?

She hoped that everything had blown over by now and he would accept that he'd acted like a fool. She looked at her phone to see if he'd replied yet, but he hadn't. Amber sighed. She heard a knock at her door.

"Can I come in for a second?" Trevor entered her office, staring at her with puppy dog eyes.

"Listen, Trev—"

"Amber, I just wanted to tell you that you can't get pregnant by me. I was in an accident when I was younger. I just wanted to say that so you don't feel no way about me." Trevor quickly turned around and walked out before she could muster up any words.

Amber sat there in thought. *Well, if that's so, then it's all good and I don't have to worry about a thing. Now, it would be bad if I wanted his . . .*

Amber's phone rang loudly, and she jumped. She looked at the caller ID; it was Stephen.

"I'm sorry, Stephen," Amber said immediately.

"I acted like a jerk. I should be the one apologizing. . . ." Stephen's voice was almost at a whisper.

"I think I know what we need. . . . A vacation. How does that sound?"

"Ummm . . . maybe you're right. I have been working like a dog, but we can't go for long. What about we go to the Keys for a long weekend?" Stephen asked, hoping she wouldn't want to go anyplace else.

"Sweetie, we always go to the Keys." Amber's voice became childlike. "Can we go somewhere else, pretty please?"

"I hate it when you beg . . . ," Stephen said, annoyed.

"Okay, I guess we can go to the Keys, like we usually do. No need for you to get upset. I'm beginning to think that you really don't want to be seen with me. You always take me to the Keys," Amber whined.

"Please don't say that. . . . I just love it there. Don't we always have a good time there?" Stephen flipped the direction of the conversation.

"Well . . . yes, we do. We sure do. . . . Will you make the arrangements?" Amber smiled while memories filled her mind.

"Can you make them?"

"Well . . . can I have your credit card number, then?" She heard laughter in the background.

"You can you use yours, and I will give you the cash later. I have another call coming in. I have to go. Love you. Talk to you later." Stephen quickly hung up the phone, not wanting to be bothered with any money questions.

"Well, I guess I will talk to you later, too," Amber said, staring at the phone, irritated by Stephen's quick dismissal. She was even more annoyed that she had to use her own money. She knew he wouldn't pay her back. *I guess I just gotta suck it up and make it work. He's the right one for me,* Amber thought.

Amber quickly typed on her keyboard to locate their favorite resort out in the Keys, Casa Marina. She simply adored the style of simplicity at the hotel. Everything was at your fingertips, but of course, it came with a pretty hefty price tag. She snatched her wallet from her purse, pulled out her credit card, and booked the room for the weekend. She waited a long time for the confirmation. After ten minutes it finally came through to her in-box.

At first, she thought something was wrong with her credit card. She had been going back and forth with representatives from three different companies concerning charges on her card that she didn't make. She made a mental note to ask Stephen about her pending check from her second investment.

Amber yanked her cell phone off the desk and dialed. "Hello. Do you have any info for me?"

"Can you meet me in thirty minutes?"

"Same place?" Amber quickly asked while gathering her purse.

"Yes," said a deep voice.

Amber walked into the restaurant with only a minute to spare. She remembered her father telling her that once he'd been late to a meeting and the ex-agent left. He returned all her father's money the next day. It cost her father twice as much to get the vital information the ex-agent had.

She took a seat. An envelope was placed on the table. Amber nervously took the envelope and opened it. She peeked inside and saw pictures of Stephen, but his lips were locked to someone else's. Tears filled her eyes. When she looked up, the ex-agent had left the table. She looked around to see if she could see him. Amber had questions, lots of questions. She searched for the waitress and ordered a shot of whiskey. Amber pulled out the pictures. One by one she glanced at them and denied the true fact that Stephen was a liar. She looked back in the envelope. Amber pulled out a small white sheet of paper that had been folded in half. She unfolded the note.

There are more pictures if you want them. There are some other issues that I need a few more days to uncover. I will contact you.

Amber knocked back the drink placed before her by the waitress and ordered another. She pulled out her wallet and yanked a fifty-dollar bill out. She wanted to study and analyze each picture but knew she couldn't do that. Instead, she stuffed the pictures and the note back in the envelope and then placed the envelope in her purse. The waitress returned with her drink, and again she knocked it back. Amber rose and left the money on the table and looked at the waitress. "Keep the change."

Amber's eyes started to tear, and when she reached her car, she let it all out. She sat there crying and wishing that she had never made that phone call. Amber looked in the mirror and could see her eyes were bloodshot. She reached for tissues in her purse and wiped the tears still flooding her sight. Amber glanced at the envelope in her purse and didn't want her reality to sink in. She started her car, then drove out of the parking lot and headed home.

Chapter 8

Amber felt hurt and betrayed. She wanted the life she'd dreamed of having with Stephen, even if that meant settling for his dissatisfying sex and his sleeping around. Amber didn't want to come to grips with her new reality. She couldn't imagine that all this time she has been with him he would be this sneaky and hurtful. Her king-sized bed was covered with tissues when she finally woke up the next morning. The sounds of her message alerts and missed calls continued to chime as she rose out of bed and headed to the bathroom.

She hit the light switch and felt an unsettling feeling in her stomach. Amber turned the faucet on in the sink and cupped water to her lips. When the cold water trickled down her throat, it moistened her dry mouth. She tried sipping another mouthful, but this time the water made an escape to the sink. She rushed to the toilet to empty the contents of her stomach. She was literally sick to her stomach and didn't want to move, fearing she would fall over from pure heartache.

Trevor looked at his watch. *Damn! Where the fuck is this bitch? She's always here by ten. Shit, it's damn near twelve, and she ain't showed yet. I guess I will have to stretch it out,* he thought, reaching for his phone.

It may take longer than we thought.

Ray walked into the garage and headed for Amber's office. He was surprised that she was not there. Usually, if she took the day off or was sick, she would call him. He looked at his phone, just in case he might have missed her call, but she hadn't called. He stared out into the garage and motioned for Trevor to come into the office. Ray took a seat behind Amber's desk.

Trevor walked in and seated himself, facing Ray. "What's up, boss?"

"I know your probation is up at the end of the week." Ray shifted in his seat. "Well, when you first got here, we agreed that your stay was to fulfill your probation, but . . ."

"Boss, are you trying to offer me a permanent job?" Trevor blurted out.

"Slow your row, young man. . . . There are a few things we need to clear up first." Ray put his hand up.

"Okay, so what's the deal? You know I don't like to beat around the bush, so just say whatever you got to say." Trevor eyed Ray.

Ray cleared his throat. "First, what time did you get in this morning?"

"Actually, I got here a little early . . ." Trevor said, hoping he wasn't busted.

"I see. So, tell me, is there a reason why you have been *borrowing* the company's tools?" Ray folded his hands in front of him.

Trevor was shocked by his accusation but didn't let it show. He was a quick thinker when it came to throwing game. "Yeah, I did. I got this part for my car that I wanted to install after work, but I left my ratchet set at my boy's house, so I *borrowed* the one that's here." Trevor folded his hands onto his chest. "Now, is this conversation going where I think it's going?"

"Listen, Trevor"—Ray cleared his throat and spoke calmly—"I asked you the question, and you provided the correct answer. Now, as you know, you are very skilled, and I am not sure what you want. Would you like to continue working here? Are you going to leave once this whole probation hold is lifted?"

"I see . . . I mean, it would only make sense. . . . Well, can I at least stay here for another week or so . . . ? I mean, my paperwork should be finalized by then and—"

"Then it's settled. We will revisit this conversation again once you're cleared." Ray motioned for him to go back to work. He followed Trevor out of Amber's office.

Amber's stomach wasn't turning upside down anymore. When she finally stood to her feet, she looked into her bedroom. She saw the empty Jack Daniel's bottle on the floor, staring back at her from across the room. "So, you're the fucking culprit!" She cursed herself. "Let's try this again. . . ." She turned the water on from the sink faucet. Amber splashed the cold water on her face. "That feels better," Amber said out loud, relieved of her foggy cloud. She heard the missed-call alerts from her phone. Amber ignored it but knew she couldn't hold off much longer. She shut the faucet off.

Amber slowly walked into her room and picked up the empty bottle and set it on her nightstand. She started to snatch up the crumpled tissues on her bed and throw them into the small trash can beside her nightstand. "Oh, my fucking God

. . . shut the fuck up!" Amber screamed as she searched the room for her phone. She spotted her purse and stomped over to silence the noise. Her heart sank. She pulled out the envelope that had crushed her dreams of a "happily ever after" life.

She fell to her knees and emptied the envelope's contents onto the floor. Amber counted the pictures. *Ten, eleven, and twelve . . . How could you? Am I not good enough for you? Is it my weight?* Questions ran through Amber's mind. She wanted answers but didn't want to deal with the truth.

"Amber Couture, what the fuck is wrong with you? Are you going to let some pictures destroy your dreams of having a man that's financially secure, stunningly handsome, and, above all else, liked by your father? You better get a hold of yourself and remember who the hell you are . . ." She stood in front of her full-length mirror and smoothed out her hair. "Amber Couture, independent, intelligent, sexy as hell." She tossed her hair back off her shoulders. "Accomplished and, most of all, worth more than any whore he may have on the side!" she barked out loud to herself. Amber picked up the scattered photos and placed them in her safe in her closet. "You done fucked with the wrong bitch."

***

Six months later . . .

Trevor drove a 2011 Mercedes-Benz S600 to the back for detailing. His phone vibrated. "What's up, baby?" he asked as he looked around.

"I thought you said this was gonna be over soon. What? You fucking forgot about the camera? What? You think I wasn't watching you?" a woman's voice squealed through the phone.

"Relax, baby. I got this. You don't—"

"Fuck that shit. It's 'cause of me that this shit is even going down. So don't you fucking play me. You getting your cake, ice cream, and fucking candy all at the same damn time!"

"Are you finished now? Look, we will be set for life. Just let me fucking work! Damn!" Trevor yelled into his phone.

"We fucking better be. I swear!" The call disconnected.

Good God all fucking mighty, this bitch is gonna drive my ass fucking nuts. I better come up with better plans that don't include her fucking ass. Shit! Trevor tapped his phone against his head.

"Hey, Trevor, right?" Robert's voice caught Trevor off guard.

"Yeah, yeah . . . ummm . . ." Trevor answered on edge.

"Don't worry, man. I know what women can do to a brotha. . . ." Robert laughed to lighten the awkwardness.

Trevor handed him the keys to the car and laughed as he walked away. *Damn. Now I definitely gotta get that bitch to stop calling me. She gonna fuck up my entire setup.*

Robert's eyes opened wider, as if a light bulb had flipped on. He remembered Trevor's face. Many years ago, while in New York, Robert visited a used car lot as a favor for his father. That was his first opportunity to see what one of his father's businesses was about. There was a potential investment to be made if the venture seemed lucrative. He remembered walking onto the car lot and immediately halting at the sight of a two-hundred-pound-looking Rottweiler chained to the fence. He looked around and heard some loud shouts and laughter coming from behind the mobile office. Shortly after the dog stopped barking, he was approached by some young men, mostly gang affiliated. He nervously told them why he was there as a small crowd surrounded him. In the middle of his explanation, out of nowhere a young man slammed his fist against his jaw. *Bam!* Robert fell to the ground but wasn't knocked out. He struggled to get up and run. The young man hurled profanities at him and laughed at him. That young man was Trevor. At that moment he decided he didn't want any part of this business his father had.

Robert began to steam with anger. He had to watch his back with Trevor. He couldn't believe he was even working at this dealership. How in the world did Mr. Couture miss the background check on this one? he thought. *I may just have to let my sister deal with this dealership. I wouldn't want Amber to find out about the incident or get caught up in some mess.* He shook his head at the thought.

Chapter 9

Amber picked up her phone and dialed Stephen's number. "Hey, you. How are you?" She held back on the angry attitude and decided to go after what she wanted.

"Sorry, baby. I've been working nonstop. I didn't get to call you back about the dates to go to the Keys. Did you finalize everything?" Stephen asked with a sincere tone.

"I know, baby. You work hard. . . . We're leaving Thursday night, so you have about two days to wrap up whatever you got going on. Do you want to drive, or shall I just hire a limo?" Amber spoke in a fake enthusiastic tone to mask her true feelings.

"Well, you seem excited. . . . Last time we spoke, you weren't excited at all. I'm happy to see that you came around. . . . Ummm, why don't you just get the limo, 'cause I may want to get a little frisky on the way out there." Stephen laughed lightly, hoping she would get the hint.

"Oh, yes . . . only if you're good . . . This will be an unforgettable weekend, I promise. . . . I gotta go. Talk to you soon." Amber ended the call.

Damn, she never did that before, he thought. *Am I slipping? I'm always the first to give her the dial tone.* He stared at his phone and dialed a number. "My man, what's—"

"Don't fucking *my man* me. Your check fucking bounced. I want my total investment amount back. All of it, six hundred thousand dollars, in a cashier's check. FedEx it to me in four days or else," an angry voice shouted. Then the line went dead.

Stephen quickly rose from his seat and headed through his front door. *Fuck, this is the last thing I need,* he cursed to himself.

Amber arrived at the office at ten on the nose. She said her hellos to the sales department as she walked to her office.

She bumped into Robert on her way.

"Good morning. I have been trying to call you. Is everything all right?" he said.

"Everything is just fine. Thank you. I was dealing with some personal affairs. What can I do for you?" she asked, entering her office.

"Oh, okay. Well, I hope everything is good now. Ummm, there are a few things I would like to go over with you before . . ." Robert hesitated.

"What? Is there a problem? Don't tell me one of the cars is messed up? Oh, God . . ." Amber took her seat to prepare for the worst.

"No, no, nothing like that. I wouldn't let that happen under my watch," Robert assured her.

"Okay, so then, what is it?" Amber questioned.

"Well, I'm going to be leaving here soon. It's my mom. She's not well, so I'm going to have my sister take my place here. I have already brought her up to speed on everything, so she will be your contact from now on. I e-mailed you all of her contact information," Robert lied.

"Wow, I'm so sorry to hear that. Can I do anything for you?" Amber asked sincerely.

"No, it will be . . . You know what? You *can* do something for me. I would like to invite you to dinner tonight, if you can go, of course. What do you say? I'm making our favorite. . . ."

"Ooh . . . include some sweet corn and I'm there." Amber smiled. *He's so sweet. Quitting the job to be with his mom . . . ,* she thought.

"Okay, here is the address. I will see you at seven, then." Robert walked out of the office, smiling.

Amber smiled back at him and looked at the address. Suddenly she heard a loud bang from the garage. When she looked up, she saw Trevor holding his arm to his chest. Amber rushed out of her office. "Hey, what happened?"

Trevor looked at her. "Oh, it ain't nothing. Something snapped and caught me in the arm. Ain't nothing. I can handle it."

"Go get some ice and an Ace bandage from the first aid kit out of my office. Now!" Amber spat at a coworker.

"I'm fine. No need to make a big deal out of it. Let me . . ." Trevor winced with pain.

"Do you think it's broken? Should I call an ambulance? Do you want to go home?" Amber spat questions out like rapid fire.

"Girl, don't you know who I am? I'm stronger than you think." Trevor lowered his voice to a whisper. "Don't tell me you forgot already?"

Amber couldn't help but to remember their moment. She smiled at the thought.

"Ah, so you do remember." Trevor licked his lips. When his coworker returned with the ice and Ace bandage, he wanted to slap him for moving so quickly. He snatched the ice and walked away.

"Well, a *thank-you* would have been nice," she said, loud enough for Trevor to hear. She took the Ace bandage out of the coworker's hand and walked back to her office, annoyed at Trevor's rudeness.

Amber threw the bandage on her desk as she took a seat. She typed the words *ovulation kits* into the Google search box. Amber already knew she could get one from a local pharmacy, but she wanted to make sure it was an accurate test. She searched and purchased a kit online, to be delivered to her house the next morning.

Yeah, I got something for your ass. You ain't going to treat me like some regular old chick. I plan on being in your life for forever. She wanted a permanent place in Stephen's heart, and this was the way to stay.

Chapter 10

Stephen entered the bank and went straight to the manager. "We have a problem."

The short, bald-headed, middle-aged man rushed him into his office and closed the door. "Stephen, you know we can't talk here. What the fuck are you thinking?"

"Listen, one of the investors said his check bounced, and he wants all his investment money back. Six hundred thousand in a cashier's check to him in four days." He counted out loud the days of the week. "That's fucking Monday morning. What the fuck are we going to do?" Stephen was in a panic.

"Calm the fuck down. I will fix it. Just send me the address of where the check has to go. Now, get the fuck out, and next time, do me a favor and call me first so I can meet you outside somewhere."

"Just fucking fix it. I'm leaving tomorrow night and won't be back till Monday night." Stephen spoke with irritation.

"Yeah, well, you better see about making up some of that money we are about to lose. Now leave." The middle-aged man's face was turning red with anger.

Stephen walked out of his office, thinking of from whom and where could he get anywhere close to six hundred thousand dollars. *Amber, baby, I guess you're right. It will be an unforgettable weekend, after all.* His thought brought a smile to his face. His mood changed for the better. He stopped at a bar close to the bank. He ordered two shots of Scotch and knocked them back. Stephen sat there for an hour, plotting his escape.

Amber glanced at her watch and couldn't believe that it was already five o'clock. She logged off her computer and reached for her purse to head out of the office for the day. She grabbed the slip of paper with Robert's address on it and read it. *Hmmm, for a man that doesn't know great champagne, he sure does live in a posh neighborhood,* she thought, slipping the paper into her purse. When Amber reached the doorway, Trevor was standing there, holding his arm.

"I wanted to say thanks for earlier. Would you mind helping me wrap my arm, please?" Trevor eased by her into her office, took a seat, and held out his arm.

"Ha, you got some nerve. It ain't me you gotta thank. It's your coworker," Amber blurted out.

Trevor looked through the glass and noticed everyone had cleared out of the garage. He needed this to work. "Yeah, I eventually did." Trevor reached for her and pulled her between his legs. He stared into her eyes and gently slid his hand up her skirt.

"Now, I thought you wanted me to wrap your arm up?" She opened her legs slightly and tilted her head back. "Don't start anything you can't finish." Amber let out a soft moan and couldn't resist his touches. Thoughts of Stephen crossed her mind for a quick moment. *Okay, so if you can't make it happen, then someone can always fill in for you now and then. I can certainly get my cake and ice cream with lots of toppings.* Suddenly, her cocky attitude took over. "You are going to fuck me . . . right now. . . ." Amber ripped his shirt open and aggressively motioned for him to unzip his pants.

Trevor's face flashed a quick smile once her motives were clear. She couldn't have played her role any better for him. He glanced quickly at the tissue box on her desk and moved into a position so that his face was out of view. He knew that he already had footage of the other day, so he would just have his girl edit it and make everything look good. When he first began his probation, this plot wasn't easy to maneuver. His girlfriend of two years was the one who put the plan into motion when she started going to film school.

Amber's breasts bounced up and down as she rode him. "Oh, yes. . . . pull my hair. . . . Suck on my nipples. . . ."

Trevor did as he was told, but hesitated with his movement to put a show on for the camera. "Is this what you want, Ms. Couture?"

"Yes . . . this is what I want. . . . Just sit there until I'm done." Amber's body moved faster.

"Would you fire me if I were to stop?" Trevor held on to her ass and slammed her harder with each bounce.

"Ooh . . . fuck." Amber placed her hands on her breasts and caressed them.

"Ms. Couture, will you fire—"

Amber stopped all movement and was in his face. "Yes, I will. Now, shut up and fuck me. I don't have time for this Q & A bullshit. Just do what you do best."

Trevor got the message loud and clear. He figured those words had just sealed the deal. Her hands wrapped tighter around his body as he stood up and placed her on her desk. Trevor made a quick sweeping motion with his hand, clearing some paperwork, along with the box of tissues, on her desk. He knew from this point on there was no holding back. Trevor made sure the only sounds that were heard were her bliss.

Amber sat in her car, looking at a huge gate that led to a castle-like estate. She was amazed and almost wished she had picked up on his offer sooner. When she first looked at the address, she noticed it was in Miami Beach, but when she punched it into her GPS, she couldn't believe that Robert lived on Star Island. This exclusive community was known for its wealth and celebrity residences. She pressed a button. The gate buzzed and started to open. As she drove in, she could see someone standing outside the main house, waiting for her. The property was vast and had the beach as its backyard. There was one enormous house, then two other houses on each side, with beautiful flowers and tall palm trees all around. She stepped out of her car and took in the breathtaking view for a moment.

"Good evening. Mr. Polland has been expecting you," said a voice, interrupting her moment.

"Yes, I believe he is." Amber followed an older man into the main house.

As she entered the house, her eyes couldn't believe how beautiful it really was. The vestibule was an open area with marble flooring, and there was a huge vase filled with fresh flowers that scented the entrance. She saw two staircases on opposite sides leading to the top floor. She stood still for a moment.

"Mr. Polland is in the kitchen. Please, follow me this way, Ms. Couture."

She followed the older man into a gourmet kitchen. It seemed like a picture straight out of *House & Home* magazine. She saw Robert placing some corn and potatoes into a pot. He wore a short-sleeved blue polo shirt and some plaid-colored shorts. His height and weight were in perfect proportion; he was neither too big and muscular nor too slender.

"Mr. Polland, your guest has arrived. Will you need anything else?" the older man asked.

"Yes. Can you open the champagne and pour Ms. Couture a glass, please? Thank you. I'm almost done." He turned to Amber. "I'm glad to see you."

"Yes, me too." She took the glass from the older man. "So, why didn't you tell me?"

"What? That I had money?" Robert poured himself a glass of champagne as he laughed. "I would hope that it doesn't matter. Besides, I thought you had boyfriend." Robert's eyebrows rose.

"I guess it doesn't matter. Yes, I do have a boyfriend. . . ." Amber's voice trailed off.

"Okay, I get it. Let's just enjoy each other's company. I would like to think we are friends," Robert quickly interjected.

"Honestly, we are going through a little rough patch right now and . . ."

"Amber"—Robert took her hand in his—"we don't have to talk about it. I don't want any negative energy. Let's drink, enjoy this delicious seafood feast I am preparing, and forget about the other stuff. Do you like the champagne?"

"Yes, I do, and I can see you remembered my favorite." Amber smiled. She felt a connection at that moment but didn't want to act on it. She knew she couldn't, at least, not right now.

Robert put the shrimp, crawfish, crab, and andouille sausage in the pot. "Okay, so dinner should be done in about fifteen minutes. Now, would you like to eat here or outside by the pool?"

"Well, I haven't even been out back yet, so I guess by the pool."

"Okay. Let me get Walter so he can set everything up for us. That way I can give you the grand tour of the place. How does that sound?" Robert gestured with his hands in the air.

"Sounds wonderful. Let's do it," said Amber.

Robert left the kitchen to instruct Walter on his plans. Upon his return, he noticed that Amber's shoes and purse were off to the side of the entrance to the outside. He picked up the bottle of champagne and went outside to meet her. The soft light of the sky made her skin look radiant. She wore an all-white, semitransparent sundress that made her curves stand out in the best way. He stood staring at her as she watched the waves of the ocean roll in and out. He walked up behind her. "It's beautiful, isn't it? I love it here. Out of all the homes we have scattered about, this one is the best."

"Really? And how many homes does your family have? Damn," Amber said, not taking her eyes off the ocean.

"Oh, about a dozen or so in the United States, but my family also owns some resort properties abroad, like in Dubai. I love that place, too."

"My goodness . . ." Amber's jaw dropped. "For a person that is so well off, why do you still feel the need to oversee a business like detailing? I think I would have chosen to scout out more properties for potential resorts." She laughed.

"Well, this business was the very first company my family had. It goes all the way back to the forties, believe it or not. Let me put it this way. If you can't run this business, then you can't even try any other family business." Robert poured some more champagne into her glass and placed the bottle on a small table.

"I see, but I still don't understand. You told me you didn't know anything about cars."

"Well, okay, I'm caught." Robert stepped back and bowed his head in shame. "I lied. I just wanted to spend some more time with you." Robert looked up and hoped she wouldn't hold it against him.

"Wow, I guess if your mom didn't get sick, I would have never known any of this, huh?" Amber looked into his eyes. "So, are you lying about anything else?"

"Well . . . yes, I have a dragon in the basement, and his feeding time is at eight." Robert gave her a smirk.

Amber playfully pushed him off balance. "Come on. Stop it."

Robert took her hand and looked deeply into her eyes. "No, there is nothing else." He declined to tell her about his divorce.

They both stood there watching the waves roll in and continued to talk and joke around until Walter signaled them to the outside dining area for dinner. Amber nearly fell over from eating and drinking so much. When the food was great and her stress level was high, her favorite way to calm herself was by eating. Drinking champagne didn't help the situation, either. She kept her glass full of champagne so she could forget all about Stephen.

Amber couldn't help that her sexual appetite was growing. She thought Robert purposely planned this dinner with all the aphrodisiac foods and good conversation. If she didn't know any better, she would think he was definitely trying to get into her panties. Robert didn't know it, but he could have just simply tried to kiss her. She would have definitely gone all the way happily. She made a mental note. *No more seafood dinners with Robert.*

Robert decided to have someone take her home and to have another member of his staff followed them with her car. He'd noticed that they drank about two and a half bottles of champagne, and he definitely didn't want her driving home. He did offer for her to spend the night in one of the guesthouses, but she declined. Robert understood why she didn't want to stay. They'd had some intimate moments that caused some awkward pauses. Robert himself had noticed the sexual energy in the air, but he was a gentleman and respected Amber. He also knew that if her father found out that she'd been over here, he wouldn't like it too much.

"Thank you, Robert. I really enjoyed myself. Hopefully, we can do this again." Amber smiled, looking up at him.

He kissed her gently on the cheek and escorted her to the car. "I hope we can do this again soon. I will call you sometime tomorrow to see how you're doing. Now, are you sure you don't want to spend the night? You did have a lot to drink."

"I don't think I should. Besides, I have something being delivered to my house in the morning, and I need to be there to sign for it. Thanks for everything." Before she stepped into the car, she kissed his soft lips gently.

Robert stood still, not knowing if he should kiss her back or not.

After the kiss, Amber got into the car without another word.

Chapter 11

"Are you fucking done yet?" Trevor asked.

"Can you just be patient? This is not an easy thing to do, unless you want to do it," Trevor's girlfriend shouted back. "It has to be perfect. We don't need this shit to blow up in our faces. I really don't think you want to be behind bars."

"You right, but I have to leave soon, and she won't be in on Friday. I think I should do it today. What do you think?"

"It might be a better look if you wait 'til you finish getting all your probation shit out of her father's hands," she replied.

"Oh, yeah. You see, that's why you my Bonnie." Trevor kissed her good-bye and headed to the front door.

"Oh, babes, you better not even think of fucking that bitch again. You hear me?" his girlfriend yelled out.

"I hear you," Trevor shouted back. *But that don't mean I will listen.* He snickered to himself.

***

Amber heard her doorbell ringing as she rolled out of bed. She threw her robe on and dashed for the door downstairs while yelling, "I will be right there." She finally got to the door and opened it.

"I have a delivery for Ms. Amber Couture. Can you sign here?" The deliveryman motioned to a clipboard for her signature.

She signed the clipboard but was surprised that her delivery was two dozen long-stemmed yellow roses. "Thank you," she said, reaching for the neatly wrapped bouquet.

"Have a nice day, Ms. Couture," the delivery-man replied.

"Yes, you do the same." She couldn't stop smiling. She almost dropped the bouquet just trying to get the card. She stopped after her near mishap and went in to place the vase on the table in her foyer. She pulled out the small card.

Thank you for making my night. Hope to see you soon.
Robert

Amber couldn't believe it. She wasn't stupid. She knew that he had feelings for her, but not on a romantic level. She remembered he always kept it professional. *Well, maybe . . . just maybe he could be the topping to my ice cream,* she thought, looking at the bright yellow roses. The doorbell rang again. She put the card next to the vase on the table and walked over to the door to open it.

"Good morning. I have a package for a Ms. Amber Couture. Can you sign for it?" The uniformed FedEx delivery guy handed her a small digital console for her to sign.

"Thank you." She signed and handed him back the console. "You have a nice day." She took the package from his hands and walked back into the house.

Yes, this is what I was waiting on. She quickly opened the package and pulled out a small box marked OVULATION TEST KIT. She rushed upstairs to her bathroom to take the test and put her plan into motion.

Ray walked into his dealership and headed for the garage. He looked at his watch. It read eight o'clock. As he entered the garage, he saw Trevor walking in. "Hey, Trevor. Can I see you for a moment in Amber's office?"

"Sure, boss. I will be right there," Trevor replied.

Ray Couture entered Amber's office and was shocked to see the mess. It looked as if there had been some type of altercation there. He turned to see Trevor in the doorway. "Did something happen in here yesterday?"

Trevor's eyes widened. "No, nothing that I know of."

"Well, okay. I will check this out in a while." He turned to Trevor and motioned for him to sit down. "As per our conversation at the beginning of the week, you were supposed to make a decision. Have you decided?"

"Well, to tell you the truth, I still haven't decided. Did you send in the final paperwork to my probation officer?" Trevor asked.

"Actually, I sent it yesterday. He should receive everything today. Is that what's holding you back from making your decision?" Ray questioned with his eyebrows raised.

"Something like that. But my decision is—"

Ray cut Trevor off at the sight of Amber walking in from the garage. "Amber, what happened here?"

Amber eyed Trevor, not knowing what had been said. "Oh, nothing happened. Why?" She quickly started to pick up some papers and her tissue box off the floor.

Ray turned to Trevor. "We will have to talk about this on Monday. Maybe we can go for lunch."

"Yeah, sure. No problem. Talk to you then, boss," Trevor quickly stated and rushed out the door.

Ray turned to Amber. "Amber, honey, is there something you need to tell me?"

"Dad, nothing is going on. I promise you. My office is a mess 'cause I was looking for a small piece of paper and just got frustrated when I couldn't find it." Amber smiled to allay her father's concerns.

"Okay, if you say so. Ummm, why are you here so early, anyway? You're never here before ten." Ray eyed the tissue box and noticed it wasn't the standard one that every exec had on their desk.

"Oh, my God, Dad, is it so bad that I came in a little early today? Oh, I may have forgotten to mention to you that Stephen and I are headed for the Keys this weekend. We decided to leave tonight and won't return until Monday night. You okay with that?" Amber playfully questioned.

"That's fine. Are you staying at the usual place? Okay, are you sure there's nothing I should know about?" Ray brought the issue up again. He felt uneasy after seeing Amber's office. He wasn't sure what was happening, but he knew his daughter was lying.

"Yes, we will be at the usual place. Dad, there is nothing happening. Please, leave it alone. So what? My office is a mess. I think you know me well enough to know the mess won't last." Amber hinted at her annoyance with her rhetorical questions.

Ray put his hands up to signal his retreat. "Okay, Amber, I guess I will see you on Tuesday. Have a safe trip, and don't forget to enjoy yourself." He walked out of her office and headed to his. There was a phone call he needed to place.

Stephen looked at the certified check in the amount of six hundred thousand dollars. He placed it into his jacket pocket and entered the building. He took the elevator to the fourth floor and stepped off. The receptionist greeted him with a smile as he pushed the double glass doors open.

"Hi. Can you tell me if Timothy Terk is in his office?"

"Give me one second, sir. Who, may I ask, is here to see him?" She picked up the phone and punched a few numbers on the dial pad.

"Stephen Hunter. Thank you," he said with a smile.

"Sir, you can go ahead to his office." The receptionist smiled again.

Stephen walked directly to his office. He didn't bother with the formalities; he just laid the check in front of him. "I would appreciate it if you don't mention this mishap to anyone else. If you do, just remember our contract of confidentiality. I would get double of what you have in your hands." Stephen walked out without waiting for a reply.

He left the building and pulled out his cell phone. "Okay, I just dropped it off. When I get back, we need to talk." Stephen hung the phone up.

Ray Couture sat at his desk and admired the picture of his deceased wife. He smiled, remembering the good times he'd had with her. His phone buzzed. "Yes, Brenda?"

"There's a Mr. Harold Rice on the line for you." Her voice projected clearly.

"Okay, please send it through." His phone rang, and he picked up the receiver. "Can you meet me in thirty? There's some business we need to discuss."

"I will see you at the usual spot," Mr. Rice answered.

***

Trevor walked into Amber's office around midday. "Sorry about earlier. If I would have known that your father wanted to speak to me in—"

Amber cut him off, annoyed. "Don't worry about it. I took care of it."

"Wow, what's the problem? What's up with the attitude?" Trevor was surprised.

"Listen"—Amber looked around to make sure no one was around and stepped closer to Trevor—"whatever you thought we had is over, and it won't happen again. So please, don't approach me on that level. If it ain't business, then you shouldn't feel the need to waltz into my office. Now, if you don't mind, I would like to finish my work."

"Yeah, okay, if that's the way you want it, Ms. Couture." Trevor calmly walked out. He pulled out his phone and sent a text message.

Babes, my paperwork is with the probation officer. Are you finished?

Trevor's phone buzzed with a new text message.

So we in the clear. It's done.

Trevor replied, Send the copy. This bitch done tested the wrong one.

Will do.

Trevor smiled at the response.

Amber was sitting at her desk, wrapping up her last e-mail, when she heard a knock at her door again. Without looking up, she said, "Trevor, I told you . . ." She glanced up, and to her surprise, it was Stephen. "Honey, what are you—"

Stephen cut her off with a deep kiss. "I finished early at the office, so I thought we would get a head start. What do you say?"

"Well, let me finish this up. It will take me a minute. Why don't you say hello to my dad? I'm sure he would like to see you. From what I hear, you two haven't golfed in weeks."

"Your dad isn't in. I checked before I came to your office. Maybe I will just check out what you guys have in the showroom. I'll wait out there for you," Stephen replied.

Amber rushed through her last e-mail response and clicked the SEND button. Another e-mail appeared in her in-box, but she didn't recognize the sender. She thought of spamming the message but decided to leave it unread. She logged off her computer and grabbed her purse.

As she walked through the garage and passed Trevor, he mumbled, "You need to look at that message." His devious smile made her uneasy.

Amber stopped but said nothing. She made a mental note. *How the fuck does he know I didn't look at a message?* His words made her curious, but not enough to delay her fun-filled weekend. She strutted into the showroom with smiles and almost leaped into Stephen's arms. "Okay, let's go, babes. I'm ready."

Stephen squeezed her curvy body tightly. "Hey, do you think your father would give me a good deal on this 2011 Bentley Mulsanne?"

"If you play your cards right this weekend, you just may get an even better deal from me." Amber kissed him and gestured to leave.

"Sounds like I better start playing now." Stephen grabbed her by the hand and walked out of the dealership. He knew his weekend would have to be a productive one. His mind was on the money—her money. He knew if this weekend went well, he could make up at least a quarter of the six hundred thousand. Upon his return, he could make his moves to branch out.

Chapter 12

Ray rushed to the table as he glanced at his watch. He had exactly two minutes to spare. He surely didn't want to be late. The last time he was late, it cost him a lot more money.

"So, Ray, what can I do for you?" Mr. Harold Rice sipped on a cup of coffee.

"Remember about two years ago? I came to you to look into someone named Trevor Turner? Well, I need you to look into him again. I don't know what's going on there, but my gut is telling me I have to find out." Ray motioned for the waitress and ordered a glass of lemonade and a turkey club sandwich.

"I see. That shouldn't be a problem," Mr. Rice stated.

The waitress returned with Ray's lemonade and set it before him. "And . . . there's something else. . . . My daughter . . . there's something going on with her, but I can't . . ." Ray bowed his head.

Mr. Rice shifted in his seat. "Is there anything in particular you're looking for? I mean, what exactly it is you want me to . . ."

Ray held his hand up to stop him from talking. "I actually want you to look into her boyfriend, Stephen Hunter. I know you gave me a file on him when Amber started seeing him, but can you just review his file again and do a deeper search? As for my daughter"—Ray scratched his chin and stared down at the table—"I want you to see what, exactly, she has been up to. And can you look into her bank accounts? I want to know what her finances look like."

The waitress appeared with Ray's turkey club sandwich and placed it in front of him. She offered Mr. Rice another cup of coffee and Ray another glass of lemonade. They both declined and thanked her. She retreated back to the kitchen.

"Ray, about a week ago your daughter called me. She wanted me to look into Stephen. I did and still am. I can tell you that he has been quite a ladies' man. Well, just one lady, anyway. Her name was Candy."

"Wait, what do you mean, was?" Ray almost choked on his sandwich. He grabbed the glass of water on the table.

"He's not seeing her anymore. They went to New York the other week, to a party, and when they returned, he stepped off the jet immediately after it landed, but Candy . . . she didn't get off until an hour later. I have pictures of her leaving the jet in an overcoat and stumbling on the taxiway." Mr. Rice took his last sip of coffee.

"So, why is my daughter going away with him this weekend?" Ray said out loud. "Did you show her the pictures?" Ray asked.

"Yes, I did, and when I did meet her with them, her tears instantly appeared."

Ray held up his hand again, not wanting to hear the rest. He pushed his plate to the side. "You mentioned that you were still looking into him. Have you found out anything else?"

"Funny you say that. He doesn't have a real office. He uses a friend's office in downtown Miami. The companies that he has been consulting for and investing for are all dummy companies. This hedge-fund broker title is all a scheme. He has no intentions on paying out on any investments." Mr. Rice filled his ear.

"Have you contacted her with this info?" Ray questioned.

"Yes, several times, but it seems that she turned her phone off."

"She's staying at . . . at . . . fuck, I can't remember the name, but you can search her credit card statements. She always goes there when she goes to the Keys. Thanks, Harold." Ray dropped a fifty-dollar bill on the table and left.

Oh, my God, what should I do? If I go to her with this information, she will know I have been checking up on her. I don't want any strain on our relationship again. That's what happened last time, when she discovered that I had all her ex-boyfriends looked into. Ray's thoughts crammed his mind.

Chapter 13

Amber straddled Stephen as soon as the limo started to move down the driveway. She'd taken the ovulation test earlier that morning, and it had shown positive. Her mind was on one thing only—sex—and she wanted it every possible way. *I will make you forget all about that blond bitch,* she thought. She'd worn Stephen out over the last four days and nights.

The limo pulled into her driveway and stopped at her door. Stephen stepped out of the limo first, then helped Amber out. He allowed the limo driver to bring her bags to the front door. Stephen looked at her and kissed her gently. "That was a great time. We have to do that again. I never knew you had all that sexual energy bottled up inside of you."

"Wait, aren't you coming in?" Amber quickly interjected.

"Sweetie, I will be back tomorrow. I have to handle some business affairs. You know I have

been gone for four days, and it really doesn't
matter that it was a weekend." He held her close.
"Now, baby, we just came back from a fantastic
weekend. Let's not ruin it by fighting. I promise I
will see you tomorrow. Okay?"

Amber kissed him on the lips. "You're right. I
guess I will see you tomorrow. Well, at least call
me when you're finished." Amber reached for
her keys to unlock the front door.

Stephen motioned to the limo driver to place
Amber's bags into the foyer. He kissed Amber
good-bye, then hopped back into the limo. The
driver rushed to the driver's side and got in. Amber watched the limo drive out of her driveway,
then out of view.

Amber went into the house and immediately
went to her bathroom and pulled out a pregnancy
test. She laughed at herself. *Now, you know
there's no way in hell you could be pregnant,*
she thought. Her scheme of getting pregnant by
Stephen, to keep him around, would surely take
longer than a long weekend of hot sex. She placed
the test back in the medicine cabinet. She thought
of calling Stephen but decided it would be best
if she waited for his call. She unpacked her bags
and watched a rerun of *Fatal Attraction,* then fell
asleep in her bed.

The next morning Amber awoke earlier than usual. It was six o'clock. She didn't have to be at work until ten. She tried going back to sleep, but she tossed and turned. Amber finally got off the bed and headed into the bathroom for a shower.

After getting dressed and applying her makeup, she took her cell phone out of the nightstand drawer, powered it on, and set it on top of the nightstand. Amber headed downstairs to the kitchen. She put on the coffeemaker, took a mug out of the cabinet, set it on the counter, and went back upstairs.

Before reaching her bedroom door, she could hear the missed-call alerts blaring from her phone. Damn, I forgot to check my voice mails last night, she thought. She let out a sigh, grabbed her phone, and shut off the alerts, then threw it into her bag and walked downstairs.

She placed her pocketbook on the counter, then poured her coffee and sweetened it. After a few sips of coffee and daydreaming about Stephen, she reached for her phone. As she looked through her missed-call list, she noticed that the ex-agent had called her a number of times. He didn't leave a message. She took a deep breath. "Do I really want to know about any more of his affairs?" she asked herself out loud. "Have I forgiven him?" she continued. "Do I still want this future with him?" She stared blankly at the phone.

"Good morning, Ray. How have you been?" Robert asked, entering the office.

"Oh, just been hanging in there. You know what I mean." Ray fidgeted and walked to his window. He could see all the employees that had entered the grounds.

Robert noticed Ray's antsy movements. "Ray, is everything okay?"

"I can't answer that honestly, so I'd rather not say," Ray spat.

"I don't mean to intrude, but there are a few things I would like to go over with you before my sister takes over fully."

Ray's phone buzzed. "Yes, Brenda?"

"Trevor Turner is here to see you."

Ray looked at his watch. Eight thirty, it read. He rubbed his chin, then spoke. "Brenda, can you tell him I'm in a meeting? But set up a one o'clock reservation for lunch at P.F. Chang's on Biscayne Boulevard. And, Brenda, tell Trevor to show up at two. Got it?"

"Yes, Mr. Couture." Brenda did what she was told.

"I hope she doesn't screw that up." Ray let out a nervous laugh.

"Ray, if you like, we could go over this later."

"I know my daughter came to your house the other night. Is there something you need to tell me?" Ray looked at Robert with haste.

Robert tilted his head back and formed a wrinkle in his forehead. "Mr. Couture, I think you have it all wrong. After I finished talking to you about my future plans that day, I went to give Amber a heads-up. I might have lied to her about the reason I was leaving just to get the date, but after that night . . ." Robert sat up straight and looked directly into Ray's eyes. "Mr. Couture, while working with your daughter, I actually got to know her a bit. So, I invited her to my house for dinner and drinks that night. That's all. Now, if you're asking me what happened there between us, that's a different story."

"Don't you dare. That's why I stopped doing business with your family a long time ago! I know what the fuck you think you're trying to do. What? You think you can cozy up to my daughter to acquire some of our properties? I know what your family really does."

"Now, let's not go there, because I'm sure all the crap that you have heard is not all facts. Just like you want to protect your family's business, so do I. My father isn't around to help me or tell me which way to stir the pot. So, understand that I do not want any of your properties. If it would make you feel better, we can cut ties now business-wise."

"I think that would be best. If your feelings are genuine for my daughter, then you shouldn't have anything to do with her bread and butter. I'm sure you understand what I mean." Ray put his hand out to shake Robert's.

"Sorry, it didn't work out, Ray. Who knows? It may work out another way down the line." Robert shrugged. "Ray, since we no longer have a business relationship, I guess I can ask you this one thing that's been bugging me."

"Yeah, but just remember whose father I am." Ray gave him a small smirk.

"That mechanic, Trevor Turner, did you forget to do the necessary background check on him or what?" Robert gave a light chuckle.

"What the fuck you think this is? Some type of a toy store or some shit? You don't think I would do the proper background check? I think you are underestimating me. I know what I'm doing, and I also know what I'm gonna do!" Ray stood at the doorway, gesturing Robert out the door.

Before Robert walked out, he casually said to Ray, "I hope you know he's gang-affiliated and probably has grand larceny charges a mile long."

"Listen here, son. I was in this business way before you were an itch on your father's balls. A man like me does his homework, trust me." Ray stood in front of his receptionist, Brenda.

"Good day, Mr. Couture. Hopefully, I will see you around." Robert stepped down the hall.

"Brenda, please call the locksmith and alarm company. I want new locks and new codes for all entrances by the end of the day. Thanks," Ray instructed. "Oh, when my daughter comes in, please have her call me."

Chapter 14

Amber pulled into her reserved parking spot and stepped out of her car. With her breakfast in hand, she strolled down to her office. When she entered the garage, she noticed that Trevor wasn't in. *Well, thank goodness I don't have to deal with that today,* Amber thought, waltzing into her office.

She took her seat at her desk and logged on to her computer. Amber opened the McDonald's bag containing her favorite breakfast: sausage, egg, biscuit, and two hash browns, along with grape jelly. Her mouth watered at the sight while she squeezed the jelly onto the biscuit. She closed her eyes on her first bite and savored the warm, sweet taste. As she continued to eat, her computer chimed. She had an unread e-mail.

Amber opened the e-mail without even looking at the sender's name. A video began to play. She heard her voice. "Now, shut up and fuck me. . . ." Amber couldn't believe what she was seeing on

her screen. *That motherfucker!* She knew exactly
what it was. She hadn't thought that he would
try to blackmail her. She hadn't thought that he
was that smart. She covered her mouth with her
hands and closed her eyes, fighting the stream
of tears. She wanted to throw up. Amber didn't
know how she would get herself out of this. Her
phone buzzed. She grabbed it and saw a new text
message come in.

> Meet me in the parking lot of Starbucks in
> fifteen minutes.

With her phone in hand, she picked up her
bag and ran out to her car. She sped out of the
parking lot, almost hitting an incoming car. She
knew who to look for when she pulled into the
lot of Starbucks. She searched all the outside
seating, then went inside. She saw Trevor and a
young woman sitting together. She walked over
slowly and took a seat.

"Hey, Amber. How you doing this morning?"
Trevor asked, surprised. "Didn't I tell you to
meet me in the parking lot?"

"You know exactly how I'm doing this morning," Amber spat back. "What? You didn't want
me to see your little coconspirator?"

"Okay, I guess you are right. I do know how
you doing this very fine morning. You know how
this works, I'm sure. I want one million depos-

ited into this offshore account by the end of the day." Trevor put a small slip of paper with some numbers on it in front of her.

Amber looked at it and laughed in his face. "So what? Am I supposed to be scared? Stupid hood nigga. I should have known not to fuck with you."

"Who the fuck you calling hood, bitch?" Trevor's girlfriend jumped in her face.

Trevor grabbed his girlfriend by the waist and pulled her back down in her seat. "Shut the fuck up, and let me handle this shit. Go fucking wait in the car," he grunted through his teeth. She did what she was told.

"Like I said, hood, bitch," Amber nonchalantly said to her as she left the table.

Amber reached into her bag for her iPad. "Trevor I get it. You want money, but guess what? The amount you want, it won't happen," she continued. "If you think you can file a suit against me, then go ahead. I doubt it will get far. My father knows a lot of people in high places. So, let's handle this like businessmen, as they say. I will offer you two hundred thousand, and you hand over all the copies and the original of that little film school video you put together. Because, I am sure, with all my money, I can find an expert to say that that video was created to show only certain things."

Trevor chuckled slightly and paused. He knew what she said was true, but he still wanted the money—any amount of money. "Okay, make it a half a million and I turn over everything to you, along with getting out of Miami. You go your way, and I go mine." Trevor folded his hands on his chest and sat back in his seat.

Amber looked deeply into his eyes. She quickly thought about the money in her trust. She knew dropping half a mil wouldn't hurt her. She had over twelve million in her trust, even with the money she'd invested with Stephen. Amber opened her iPad and powered it on. She looked at the slip of paper and punched in the numbers on it. Amber showed Trevor the screen. "Now, I want every single SD card, video, and the hard drive off the computer you created the masterpiece on. If it's not on my desk by"—Amber saw that it was ten thirty on her watch—"three o'clock, you can kiss that money and your freedom good-bye."

"Then our business is done." Trevor removed his sunglasses from the table and placed them over his eyes. "Have a good life, Ms. Couture."

"Oh, and, Trevor, make sure I don't have to put your little hood chick in her place, 'cause it won't go down like this. It will be very different."

Amber placed her iPad in her bag and removed herself from the table, heading for the exit. Her phone began to sound an alert. She pulled her phone out of her bag and noticed that it was an e-mail alert. She glanced at the small screen and then figured that she would just look at it when she got back to the office. She pulled out of the parking lot and headed back to the office.

"Okay, is everything set for the transfer?" Stephen asked.

"Yeah, everything is all set. Did you set everything up on your end?" the bank manager asked.

"I'm heading to the taxiway now. I will talk to you in about a month," Stephen said into the phone, then hung up. He looked around his apartment, then walked into his bedroom, where his hidden safe was. Stephen punched in the code, and it popped open. He reached in and pulled out fifty thousand dollars in cash, along with some passports and paperwork. He shoved everything into a knapsack and walked to the front door. He turned around and scanned the apartment again. "Well, it's time I moved on," he said out loud, stepping out the front door.

A taxi pulled into the driveway, and as he jumped in, his phone sounded. Stephen instructed the driver to head to Miami International Airport and looked at his phone. The transfer was complete, and his account now had over ten million in it. He smiled as he sat back in his seat and enjoyed the sun beaming on his face.

Chapter 15

Ray sat patiently waiting for Harold. For the first time, he was the early one. His watch read 12:50. He ordered a shot of Scotch, hoping it would calm his nerves. He could spot Harold coming out of the restroom area. He laughed to himself. As Harold took his seat, Ray said, "How is it you still here before me? And here I thought I had you beat for the first time in twenty years." Ray continued to chuckle, then took the last sip of Scotch.

"Because, Ray, I'm good at what I do." Harold also laughed.

"Now, tell me what you have." Ray looked at the folder that Harold's hands were on top of.

"You might need another drink," Harold said with a serious tone. He then motioned for the waitress to take their order.

For the next twenty minutes Harold informed Ray of all the mess Trevor and his girlfriend were up to.

"Harold, did she buckle to his threats?" Ray asked.

"Well, it seems that she paid him off, and I doubt that he will show up here today. She transferred a half million dollars into an offshore account in his girlfriend's name. My surveillance informed me that he is on a plane headed for Puerto Rico. There is nothing indicating that he will be back. They flew out on a one-way ticket and have left their place empty. Sorry, Ray," Harold offered.

"Well, she handled it, and she paid for her mistake. Hopefully, she learned her lesson," said Ray.

"But we have a serious problem with Stephen. Apparently, he has disappeared—"

Ray cut him off. "What's so fucking bad about that? It seems to me that he solved our problems for us." Ray smiled, but it quickly became clear that Stephen's disappearance wasn't a good thing.

"Ray, before I tell you, I want you to know that I have already taken all the steps to find his ass. And I have spoken to all your lawyers that will be involved in this."

"Lawyers . . . What the fuck are you talking about?" Ray raised his voice in anger.

"Ray, your daughter's trust fund has been wiped clean. This son of a bitch was taking money from your daughter after just three months of them dating. Now you—"

"Why didn't you catch that shit? That's what I pay you for." Ray slammed his fist on the table, catching all the patrons' eyes on him.

"Ray, you need to calm down. The only reason I didn't catch it was because you stopped the investigation of him. Remember?" Harold showed him a copy of the bank transfer on Amber's account. "This is much bigger than some dummy companies. He's into something major that includes a bank manager and good baiting and switching skills. This bank manager would take the investment checks and open an account in the check writer's name, then transfer a little at a time into the new account under an alias, in this case Stephen Hunter. So, anyone can transfer the money once they have the pass codes, and just like that, one touch from a keyboard anywhere in the world, and he's a rich man." Harold shifted in his seat and looked at his watch.

"So, can't we go to the bank manager and shake him down for the info on where this so called Stephen is?" Ray grew concerned.

"It's not that simple. We have nothing on the bank manager. Despite all my efforts, I haven't been able to figure out his true identity. What-ever identity he is using it all matches up. His pa-per trail is clean. That's why he's been the bank manager there for the last year. But my sources tell me that his identity only looks good on pa-per. That only tells me one thing, he's dirty." Harold let out a sigh.

"So, I have . . . no, my daughter has lost over ten million dollars, huh? Why doesn't she ever just listen to me? I told her just listen, dammit," Ray stormed, voicing his anger.

"Ray, what do you want me to do?" Harold asked.

"I want you to find that no-good thieving bastard, and after you get my money back, you put—"

"I understand, Ray," Harold said, cutting him off, and eased out of his seat.

Ray sat there, trying to drink his problems away. He couldn't believe what he had just heard. Most of all, he couldn't believe how stupid his daughter was. He gulped down another shot of Scotch and placed two one-hundred-dollar bills on the table and headed out the door.

Trevor and his girlfriend sat in first class for the first time. He placed his hand on her lap and smiled at her.

"What you smiling about?" she asked.

"Oh, only that we are one of those people now. No more holding on to a week's check and stretching it for two. Now I can . . . we can afford what we want at any moment," Trevor said as the flight attendant offered him a glass of champagne.

She looked at the flight attendant and asked for a glass as well. Once her glass was in her hand, she tapped it against Trevor's. "Now, baby, you have to understand we are not even close to being one of those people. That amount of money is not enough. We need more to get to where we need to be. That's why . . . I took the liberty to reach out to an old friend to help me make some new connections to invest *our* money." She smiled.

"Well, you know best, but you better make sure that those investments turn out to be lucrative."

"Trust me, this is a friend of a friend, and I have been researching this for a little while now. So, once we get to Puerto Rico, he is supposed to stop by the hotel to run through everything with us. No need to worry." She kissed him passionately and called out to the flight attendant for more champagne.

Trevor smiled but didn't trust her with all his cash. She was hood, and he knew no hood chick could ever leave the hood. He continued to smile and enjoyed his glass of champagne.

Chapter 16

It was strange for Amber to not take lunch, but today she decided to call lunch in. She called the reception area and asked if any lunch orders had been placed yet. The young lady replied no. Amber instructed her to order a tuna sandwich with tomatoes on a toasted roll and a bottle of lemonade. Amber looked at her watch. It read two o'clock. She was uneasy. Amber knew that her business with Trevor was still not complete.

Her computer chimed an alert for a new e-mail. Consumed with covering up what she did with Trevor, she'd totally forgotten about the unread e-mail. Amber knew that her father couldn't find out. If he did, he would disown her or, at the very least, move her to another dealership. She shook the thought away and looked at the new e-mail. The sender was from her bank. She opened it up and let out a loud scream. "Noooo!"

She looked at the screen, which read $0.00 FUNDS. Tears filled her eyes. She logged on to her account and saw all her bank accounts had been completely emptied. She had nothing, only what she had in her wallet. She called Stephen, but his cell phone was disconnected. She called his office and again got the disconnection message. She tried to e-mail him, and her e-mail bounced back. At that moment she felt helpless and sobbed. She'd had everything she wanted, but she had to cross the line and want more. Her father had always warned her about wanting more. She'd never listened.

Ray walked into her office and closed the door behind him. "Baby, what's wrong?" he calmly asked her, as if he didn't know everything.

Amber looked to him with tears streaming down her face. She couldn't say anything. She went to hug him and cried in his arms.

Ray consoled his daughter. It hurt him to do what he had to do, but this was the only way she would learn her lesson. "Amber, stop crying," Ray blurted out. "Now, why didn't you listen to me? I told you that throwing your money and pussy around would get your ass in trouble. And now it has caused problems. Major fucking problems."

Amber stood still, shocked by her father's tirade of words.

"Now, your lesson to learn isn't over yet." Ray picked up the tissue box on her desk and slammed it to the floor. It broke into pieces and revealed the hidden camera.

Amber looked at her father. "You knew? How long have you known? Weren't you going to warn me? Isn't family supposed to protect family?"

Ray didn't answer any of her questions. "Family? You tell me what you was thinking when you decided on having a boy toy within your own department. The stupid thing is that you knew he was a thug, didn't you? When he first came into this department, I told you just to keep your eye on him, and now I can see you kept more than your eye on him. Even though you were with someone already. It looks like he has been stringing you along the entire relationship."

Amber tried to speak. "But . . ."

"But fucking nothing. You had every fucking thing, and now what do you have?" Ray's voice became louder with anger.

Amber sat there in silence. Tears dripped from her face, and she didn't want to believe what she was hearing from her father's lips.

"Answer me. Goddammit!"

Amber's voice trembled as she spoke. "I don't know what to say. Can you fix it?"

"Fix it? That's your fucking problem, Amber. I'm always there to fix your fuckups. From this moment on you . . . you can forget about all the mess you have caused and get the fuck out of Miami. Go home, pack your shit, and head back to New York. I don't want to hear from you. Consider yourself on punishment."

"Daddy, I have no money. My accounts are wiped clean, as you know. How am I supposed to get to New York? What about my house, my car? Daddy, please don't do this to me," Amber pleaded with her father.

"Yeah, I know you have no money. Have you heard from Stephen?" Ray asked, avoiding her questions.

"Stephen? What does he . . . Oh, I see. Now I understand." Amber realized now how much mess she'd really caused.

"Do you understand now? Amber, do you know where he is?"

"I tried calling him, but his phone is disconnected, and his e-mail address is no longer valid. Daddy, I'm sorry. Please, don't—"

"Amber, you have to learn, just 'cause you can afford everything doesn't make you invincible to everyone around you and shit can't happen to you. Just answer me this one question. Why didn't you leave him once you found out that he was cheating on you?"

"Because I thought he was everything I wanted. I thought that if I confronted him, he would leave me. His manipulation fooled me. I thought you liked him. He was the first man I had dated in years, since I put on all this weight. I figured it was all good since you actually showed efforts to get to know him." Amber's tears began to fall again. "Oh, Daddy, this is all my fault. Now I have to suck it up and make it up to you in every way possible."

"It will be hard, but I think you need a slap of reality. You will be working at another dealership in New York, where I can keep close tabs on you. The money you earn will be the only money you have. I have a car waiting for you at the house to take you to the airport. From there you will fly to New York, and someone will pick you up from the airport. Your house will be up for sale, as well as your car. That's to recover a tiny bit of that money that you so carelessly handed over. Amber, you are still my daughter, but from now on you will follow my rules, not yours." Ray walked out of her office with a single tear in his eye.

Epilogue

One year later . . .

After she had been in New York awhile, working at her nine-to-five job, Amber's father finally came around and lifted her punishment. But he wouldn't allow her to return to Miami, and all her money was to go through him first. If she wanted to do anything, she would have to call him to let him know. She hated that she had put her father in such a situation, and herself, as a result of her stupidity.

Eventually, Ray caught up to Stephen in the Faroe Islands surrounded by the North Atlantic Ocean, near Europe. After he was found and all of Amber's money was returned, with a hefty fine to cover interest lost, Stephen was handed over to the CIA, courtesy of Harold Rice.

Trevor and his girlfriend got swindled out of all their money in the end. The investments that his girlfriend made panned out and turned out to be part of one of Stephen's schemes. Trevor returned to New York without his girlfriend, needless to say. His new life consisted of drugs, guns, and hoes—the life of a true gangster.

Robert searched for Amber after he returned to the Miami dealership to mend his relationship with her father. He got word of where she was and what had really happened to her. After working with her for months and trying to respect her father's boundaries was damn near impossible. He had never lost his feelings for Amber, and still wanted to be with her, even after hearing about her stupid mistakes in making her family vulnerable.

"Hello. How are you?" Robert asked.

"Why are you calling me? How did you get this number?" Amber quickly asked.

"Your father gave it to me. I just wanted to say how sorry I am for everything that happened to you."

"Robert, please, there is no need to rehash painful mistakes that could have cost my family its fortune," Amber said.

"Yeah, well, I spoke to your father, and he said it would be okay if I gave you a call and . . ."

"You're in New York?"

"Yes."